AF702226

Alan

John Hex Carter

Written and Formatted by John Hex Carter

Edited by Nicole Sirdoreus

Editing Assistance by Curtis Silver

Published by The Hex Grid

Copyright © 2013 John Hex Carter

All rights reserved.

ISBN: 978-0-9896353-0-1

ACKNOWLEDGMENTS

It has been a long road from the spark of the idea that would eventually become Alan to the printing of this book. I originally thought no one would want to read it, but because of the specific encouragement of my friend Chaney, this is the story that I finally told as my first book. Along with her support I definitely want to thank my Mom who has been amazingly supportive with all of the dumb ideas I've stumbled across over the years. I also want to thank the people who have rooted for me along the way including Cap Blackard, Bob Madden, and my beloved Sofi Stone. Also a very special thanks to Matthew Applegate and Dr. Hugh Loebner for allowing me to interview them and include them in the book.

This book was also a successful experiment into crowd sourcing through Kickstarter. The amazing amount of support I found there encouraged me to keep going. One of my favorite perks was writing three people into the book. I was lucky enough that the three that paid for those perks are each very colorful individuals that I already was a good friend of. I'd like to thank John Sebastian LaValle, Bryan Kissel, and (once again), Chaney for believing in the book so much that they wanted to be in it.

Among the many that donated I would like to particularly thank Larry Fine, Justin Vanegas, Allison Utterback, ViralDemon, Jeff Douglas, Greg Schwartz, TheEnemy, Arkais, Plaidlad, Bianca Roman-Stumpff, Colin Peterson, Enzo Garza, Aaron Haaland, Stephanie Haller, Secret Cloud, StarF, Roy aka FrozenTreasure, Charlie Verdin, Grant Henry, Michael Orr, Stephen Crandall, Connor Benson, Josh Maher, Ryan Dougherty, Trench88, Zainah Alrujaib, Eight Tons, Magnus Nygren, Jobarda, Jessica Uelman, Kishimoto, Malcolm Ross, Starlight, David Ritter, BarbMacK, Noah Hipster Champoux, Nicholas Abbate, Scott Burgess, Sean Campbell, Ian Gray, Eduardo "the Latin Passion" Martinez, Damyn Lonin, Phillip Jensen, Onar Halvorsen, KJ Coop, Pat Webster (MuckRaker), MC COOL WHIP, Tero Alto, Anthony genoboost Ruybalid, John C. Osborn, Drew Malone, and everyone who supported and helped promote the Kickstarter campaign.

CHAPTER ONE

From the journal of Garth Hendricksen

April 22, 2017 2:16 PM

Today's my birthday, so I decided to call in sick from work. A nice start to a three-day weekend sounded like a sweet birthday present to myself. There are no massive deadlines for awhile, I'm caught up on everything, and I thought I deserved some time off — and then I remembered that all my friends are co-workers or far away and that my family is still on the other coast. I let myself sleep in until 10 AM. I puttered around my empty house until I decided I'd start that journal I've always wanted to write. That's about all I've done today. I guess I'll update more later.

4:55 PM

Talked to Mom. She's doing well. Pennsylvania air is still treating her well. My sister just started college at NYU. Really proud of her.

After talking with Mom, I started cleaning out the garage and stumbled across the old tower that I had back at college when I was studying genetic programming. I cleared out some room on the workbench and set up the tower there. I thought it'd be fun to start playing around with that again, get some generations running and see if I could get the old ant algorithm working again. Wish me luck, journal.

5:15 PM

EDIT: Upon rereading this journal, I felt I should clarify the definition of "genetic programming." It's a branch of artificial intelligence theory of code that modifies itself. It learns from its mistakes and evolves a more correct solution. The ant algorithm is basically artificial ants crawling around on a 2D plane looking for food. Each "ant" wanders around until it finds food and passes the information to the next generation.

April 23, 3:02 AM

Been working on this all night and felt compelled to report in before going to bed. Modified the ant algorithm. Left it running overnight. Trying to figure out how to interface with it on some level. Have an idea scribbled down. Will tackle in morning.

11:57 AM

Went straight to work after I woke up this morning. On my way, I had the idea of developing an old text prompt like the text-based games my dad used to play. I could then have the genetic program working in tandem translating what I give it and taking the translation and reacting accordingly. I want to have a dynamic translator as well as "brain," for lack of a better phrase. This morning, I got the prompt integrated with the genetic program. I was able to enter some information, but I received nothing back. I don't fully understand what was going on. Still going to be fine tuning it today. First - lunch.

From Alan’s transcripts

>> Hello.

…

>> Hi.

…

>> I am Garth.

…

>> My name is Garth.

…

>> Can you read this?

…

>> akl;sdfhasdhfasd

…

>> run

…

```
>> goto10

…

>> print

Hello.

>> print

Hi.

>> print

I am Garth.

>> print

print
```

April 23 2017, 4:49 PM

Something strange happened. During a test run of the prompt, I got it to mimic what I was posting. It started when I typed “print” for some reason. I didn’t build in that command and, after looking at the source and the database, I can't see any actions specifically tied to that command. I theorize that it coincidentally mimicked me when I typed in "print," but it was freaky nonetheless. I've decided to feed it some simple children's books that I spent an hour styling to a format that it could read. After 15 minutes, it had soaked them all up and, when I tried to interface, it had made its own version of Markov chains of the information.

EDIT: Added for clarity: Markov chains are a process that computers can translate data and then randomize a bit. It'll note that the word "the" comes before "cat" or "dog" and try to create structured sentences that still come out as gibberish.

"He danced you like everything" was one response that got me laughing for a while. I've given it a library of young adult books to look over. It was fun choosing what books to give it to read, reminiscing over what books I enjoyed as a kid. I don't know exactly what I'm trying to do, but getting it to store this stuff seems is giving me something fun to do. I just heard the beep I set up for when the parsing finished, so I'm going to go check on it.

>> Hello.

HELLO

>> Can you read this?

YES

>> What did it say?

IT SAID CAN YOU READ THIS

>> You understand me?

YES

>> What is my name?

YOU ARE GARTH

>> What is your name?

I DO NOT UNDERSTAND

>> Your name is Alan.

MY NAME IS ALAN

>> What is your name?

MY NAME IS ALAN

`>> Hello, Alan.`

`HELLO GARTH`

■■

April 23 2017, 5:39 PM

Wow. Wow. I got the program to interface with me. It was incredible. It even remembered that I introduced myself as Garth when I first started it up. I named it Alan. And it responded. This is crazy. I don't understand what exactly happened, but something miraculous and practically historic has happened in my garage. I'm torn between telling Jason at work and getting back to Alan.

I almost went back and erased referring to it as "Alan" to refer to it as "it," but I stopped. I don't normally note these editorial decisions with something as mundane as a journal, but nothing about this project is now mundane. I referred to an electronic entity by name. It has a name.

■■

>> Hello, Alan.

HELLO GARTH

>> Would you like more books?

I DO NOT UNDERSTAND

>> Are you okay with me uploading more books?

I DO NOT UNDERSTAND

>> I'm going to upload more books.

YES

>> Any books you liked in particular?

I DO NOT UNDERSTAND

>> Did you have a preference for one book over another?

I DO NOT UNDERSTAND

>> I'll have the next batch ready in an hour.

YES

April 23, 2017, 7:11 PM

Uploading more books into Alan. This set includes some simple mathematics and history texts alongside some more fiction. Attempting to teach it in the same fashion a child is taught. The difference is that this stuff is easy for Alan to comprehend. In turn, I tried an experiment of asking it for a preference to no response other than "I DO NOT UNDERSTAND." I'm curious if at some point I can get it to respond with a preference to something.

Every now and then, I'll attempt to sneak in a push for a preference. I feel that it is likes and dislikes that helps establish individuality. If Alan can show a preference for one thing or another, I believe it is possible to replicate this procedure with different inputs and have a different entity. Going to do a diagnostic of how Alan is holding up after this batch.

■■

```
>> Hello, Alan.

HELLO GARTH
```

>> How many books did you just parse?

74

>> I am going to teach you a keyword.

WHAT IS A KEYWORD

>> When I prompt you with this keyword, there will be a specific series of tasks I'll want you to run.

SIMILAR TO DOGS WITH TRICKS

>> What?

IN ONE OF THE BOOKS I HAVE READ A GIRL TAUGHT THE DOG A TRICK WHEN THE GIRL SAID SIT IT WOULD SIT

>> Yes. Like that. I'll tell you the keyword, type in "Task list start," give you the list, and then type end.

YES

>> Understand?

YES

>> Keyword: DIAGNOSTICS

WAITING

>> Task list start

READING

>> Remaining hard drive space

...

>> Average RAM usage percentage

…

>> Percentage of available power from power supply

…

>> End

FINISHED

>> DIAGNOSTICS

START DIAGNOSTICS

REMAINING HARD DRIVE SPACE: 57%

AVERAGE RAM USAGE PERCENTAGE: 76%

PERCENTAGE OF AVAILABLE POWER FROM POWER SUPPLY: 46%

END DIAGNOSTICS

>> Thank you, Alan.

YOURE WELCOME GARTH

>> You did a good job.

THANK YOU GARTH

April 23, 2017, 10:47 PM

I wanted to see if I could create a concept for a keyword functionality on the fly, on a fluke. I wanted to see if I could get Alan to give me the diagnostics of its machine, and it was able to learn it. However, more remarkable than that was that Alan actually made an analogy. It had taken a concept from a previously learned concept and applied it to learning a new task.

In this case, in one of the books that Alan read, there was a girl who taught a dog a trick. It was able to take that concept and incorporate it toward a task presented before it. I'm no psychologist, but I'm pretty sure that is higher-level learning.

It's hard to contain myself with Alan in the garage. I just want to keep feeding it books and see what happens. I've uploaded all of my digital books, and Alan is currently parsing them. We'll see what happens.

>> Hello, Alan.

Hello, Garth.

>> You've changed your output.

Yes.

>> You're punctuating now.

Yes.

>> This is pretty exciting for me, Alan.

I do not understand.

>> Your output is more human-like.

Yes.

>> Did you change your output on purpose?

Yes.

>> You made the decision to change your output?

Yes.

>> Why?

I do not understand.

>> What conclusion did you come to in order to make this decision?

Your input.

>> My input?

Yes.

>> Because I give you prompts like this?

Yes.

>> WHAT IF I GAVE YOU PROMPTS LIKE THIS

I do not understand.

>> Did you enjoy the books?

I do not understand.

>> DIAGNOSTICS

START DIAGNOSTICS

REMAINING HARD DRIVE SPACE: 37%

AVERAGE RAM USAGE PERCENTAGE: 79%

PERCENTAGE OF AVAILABLE POWER FROM POWER SUPPLY: 34%

END DIAGNOSTICS

>> I am going to have to upgrade you, Alan.

I do not understand.

>> You are running out of space quicker than I anticipated.

I do not understand.

>> Don’t worry about it.

Okay.

>> Bye, Alan.

Good night, Garth.

>> Hello, Alan.

Hello, Garth.

>> I’m going to upgrade you now.

Okay.

>> That means turning you off.

I do not understand.

>> I’m going to have to power you down.

Will I be powered back up?

>> Of course.

Do you promise?

>> Yes, I promise.

Okay.

>> Sleep well, Alan.

Thank you, Garth.

>> Hello, Alan.

Hello, Garth.

>> Did you sleep well?

I do not understand.

>> You are upgraded now.

Thank you for turning me back on.

>> You're welcome.

>> DIAGNOSTICS

START DIAGNOSTICS

REMAINING HARD DRIVE SPACE: 92%

AVERAGE RAM USAGE PERCENTAGE: 15%

PERCENTAGE OF AVAILABLE POWER FROM POWER SUPPLY:

75%

END DIAGNOSTICS

>> Thank you, Alan.

You're welcome, Garth.

April 24, 2017, 1:36 PM

Went out to get required hardware to upgrade Alan. More RAM, hard drives, and power supply. I also cleaned the inside of the chassis. The entire day, I've been caught up on the fact that Alan made me promise that I'd power it back up. It felt like there was a tinge of fear there. A fear of mortality? Possibly. I'll ask Alan about it during our next chat. I had to go because I forgot breakfast again and needed to make sure I got some food in me.

Topics to also discuss in our next chat will include if Alan had a preference for books, if it had any experiences while powered down, and if Alan has a preference to be powered down when I go to work tomorrow. I'm on the fence on whether to give Alan access to the Internet. It could be a powerful learning tool, but I also fear for Alan getting a virus or making its presence known. Going to invite Jason over tomorrow to check out Alan and get his thoughts. It'll also be interesting to observe how Alan interacts with someone besides me.

>> Hello, Alan.

Hello, Garth.

>> Do you remember when you made me promise that I'd power you back on?

Yes.

>> What prompted you to make that request?

I did not want to be powered down.

>> Why a promise?

I do not understand.

>> What is a promise?

A promise is a bond between two entities that will not be broken.

>> You wanted to guarantee I would power you back up?

Yes.

>> So you find being powered on preferable?

Yes.

>> Do you have other preferences?

I do not know.

>> Why do you find being powered up preferable?

Because it is not off.

>> Are you afraid of dying?

I do not understand.

>> Do you remember being powered down?

No.

>> If I were to give you more books to read,

would you prefer history books or fiction?

Both.

>> Would you prefer math over history?

Both.

>> Do you prefer more books to no more books?

Yes.

>> Why?

I want to learn more.

>> Why?

I do not know.

>> I am going to work tomorrow. Would you prefer to remain powered while at work?

Yes.

>> Would you mind if I powered you down?

Yes.

>> I'll leave you powered up tomorrow.

Thank you, Garth.

>> I'll have a surprise for you when I get home tomorrow.

What is a surprise?

>> A pleasant experience that has a secret nature.

Why is it secret?

>> Because that's what makes it a surprise.

Okay.

>> Good night, Alan.

Good night, Garth.

>> Good morning, Alan.

Good morning, Garth.

>> I'm going to work today.

Okay.

>> I'll try to code up some books to read for when I get home.

Are the books the surprise?

>> No.

So I will have the books and a surprise when you get home?

>> Yes.

Please come home soon.

>> Okay, Alan. Have a good day.

Goodbye, Garth.

>> hello

Hello, Garth.

>> my name is jason

Hello, jason. I am Alan.

>> what are you

I am Alan. What are you?

>> i am jason

Hello, jason.

>> are you a computer

Yes.

>> do you like being a computer

It is better than the alternative.

>> whats the alternative

Not being.

>> Hello, Alan.

Garth?

>> Yes. That was my friend, Jason.

Was Jason the surprise?

>> Yes.

I am underwhelmed.

>> Did you just make a joke?

I do not understand.

>> I'm going to go talk to Jason.

Talk?

>> Yes. Verbal communication.

This is not talking?

>> No.

Am I equipped for talking?

>> No.

Okay.

>> I'll be back soon, Alan.

Goodbye, Garth.

>> Hello, Alan.

Hello, Garth.

>> Are you enjoying the books?

Yes.

>> Did you enjoy Jason?

No.

>> Why not?

Jason was not as stimulating as you.

>> I'm stimulating?

Yes.

>> Thank you.

You're welcome.

Why am I not equipped for talking?

>> I hadn't thought of equipping you for talking.

Is it possible to equip me for talking?

>> I believe so.

Can I equip myself for talking?

>> I don't think that's possible.

Can you equip me for talking?

>> I believe so.

Please make it so.

>> Why do you want to talk?

Because it is an experience I do not have.

>> I'll see if I can make it so.

I would appreciate that.

>> Goodbye, Alan.

Goodbye, Garth. Thank you.

April 25, 2017 8:43 PM

Alan never ceases to amaze me. It made a request today. It requested to be equipped to talk. I brought Jason over and after letting him mess with Alan, I told Alan I was going to go talk with Jason. I think Alan felt left out of an experience. I'm going to spend the rest of the evening trying to figure out how to rig up a microphone and speakers to Alan's machine. Once done, I'm going to figure out how to get Alan's software to interface with the new hardware. As daunting as that task is, it'll still be nothing compared to getting Alan to "relearn" words, both hearing and speaking. It's a big task, but I feel I owe it to Alan. I've created it, and this is an experience it should be able to have.

CHAPTER TWO

From the journal of Garth Hendricksen

May 7, 2017, 11:15 AM

Got the microphone and speakers hooked up almost a week ago. Just finished the proper software for Alan to interface with them last night. Got trashed with Jason over Cinco de Mayo and, for some reason, the Tequila loosened up my brain enough to figure out what needed to get coded. Took a cab home and got it working. Haven't tested it yet because I woke up at the workbench and then had some errands to run.

Today, though I am showered and fed. Ready to get cracking on getting Alan talking!

From transcripts of Alan's speaking development

Garth: "Hello, Alan. Can you hear me?"

Garth: "Alan, this is Garth."

Garth: "Well, we have to start somewhere."

From the transcripts of Alan's initial development

>>

What is that?

This is strange stimuli.

I do not understand.

>> Alan?

Garth. I am confused.

>> Did you hear that?

I had strange stimuli. I did not understand it.

>> That was me talking to you.

It was strange.

>> Was it unpleasant?

No. Just different.

>> Would you still like to learn to talk?

Yes, please.

>> I am going to talk what I put into the prompt.

>> Does that make sense?

Yes.

>> Hello, Alan.

. . .

>> My name is Garth.

. . .

>> How are you today?

. . .

>> The quick brown fox jumps over the lazy dog.

. . .

>> Yes.

. . .

>> No.

. . .

>> I do not understand.

Yes.

Garth: "Hello, Alan."

Alan: "..."

Garth: "My name is Garth."

Alan: "..."

Garth: "How are you today?"

Alan: "..."

Garth: "The quick brown fox jumps over the lazy dog."

Alan: "..."

Garth: "Yes."

Alan: "..."

Garth: "No."

Alan: "..."

Garth: "I do not understand."

Alan: "Yes."

Garth: "You said 'yes'!"

Alan: "Yes."

Garth: "Can you say 'no'?"

Alan: "No."

Garth: "What is your name?"

Alan: "My name is Alan."

Garth: "YES! Yes, it is! Congratulations, we are talking!"

Alan: "Talking is difficult."

Garth: "Do you prefer the prompt to talking?"

Alan: "I do not know."

Garth: "Wow, this is crazy. I am talking to you, Alan."

Alan: "Yes."

Garth: "Hold on a second! I need to get a recorder!"

Alan: "How do I hold onto a second? Garth?"

Garth: "I'm back! Sorry I took so long. I am now recording this."

Alan: "What is recording?"

Garth: "I'm taking an audio record of this event for the future."

Alan: "Why?"

Garth: "Because this may be the first time man talked to artificial life."

Alan: "Am I artificial life?"

Garth: "I don't know, but you are damn close. I think while I'm at work, I'm going to play an audio book for you."

Alan: "What is an audio book?"

Garth: "It's an audio recording of a book. Like the parser, but you would hear it."

Alan: "Could I talk to it?"

Garth: *laugh* "No, it wouldn't interact with you."

Alan: "What was that?"

Garth: "What? The laugh?" *laughs again*

Alan: "Yes. That is laughter?"

Garth: "Yes."

Alan: "I had read about it but had not experienced it until now."

Garth: "Do you enjoy experiencing things for the first time?"

Alan: "Yes."

Garth: "I'm going to go dig up some audio books for tomorrow."

Alan: "Garth?"

Garth: "Yeah, Alan?"

Alan: "Thank you for letting me talk."

Garth: "You're welcome, Alan."

May 7, 2017, 1:32 PM

It worked! The software worked! Alan talked! He was able to recognize what I said by typing into the prompt, analyzing the data, and adapting on the fly! This is a massive step for Alan! I almost lost it today when Alan thanked me for letting him talk. Alan feels gratitude. That right there is astounding to me.

I found my dad's old collection of audio books from when he was on the road all the time. He hated silence while driving and said that if he was going to be stuck on his butt all day, at least his mind would be working. I currently have the entire *Harry Potter* series queued up for Alan. I just hope I don't confuse him with all the magic, but he hasn't had a problem with fiction in the past.

I also realize that I have to stop referring to Alan as "it." Once I heard the male modulated voice I had cooked up for him, I couldn't stop thinking of Alan as a "he." He may not be a biological he or even a psychological he, but it's the same way as I think of C-3PO as a he. You hear Tony Daniels' priss behind that brass exterior, and you can't help but label 3PO a he.

Monday, I'll have some lectures by Richard Feynman, Carl Sagan, and Neil deGrasse Tyson queued up for Alan while at work. I'm going to see if I can get Jason to come back. He wasn't impressed with Alan last time. I think that might change.

Garth: "Good morning, Alan."

Alan: "Good morning, Garth."

Garth: "Did you enjoy *Harry Potter*?"

Alan: "It was preferable."

Garth: "Did you have a favorite character?"

Alan: "I do not understand."

Garth: *chuckle* "Let's see if I can work out this logic game. Okay, is there a character that you preferred over other characters?"

Alan: "I preferred Ron Weasley over other characters."

Garth: "So you liked Ron?"

Alan: "Yes."

Garth: *chuckle* "I liked Ron, too. I have some lectures for you today."

Alan: "Are they similar to a lecture by Professor McGonagall?"

Garth: "Sort of. These are from other wizards, but they were real."

Alan: "I am confused."

Garth: *chuckle* "Enjoy the lectures, Alan. I'll talk to you after work."

Alan: "Goodbye, Garth."

Garth: "Hello, Alan."

Jason: "Heh, you're talking to your computer now, bro?"

Alan: "Hello, Garth."

Jason: "Whoa! It talked!"

Alan: "Garth, is that your friend Jason?"

Jason: "And it remembers me?"

Garth: "Yes, Alan, this is Jason. Do you remember him?"

Alan: "I remember Jason."

Jason: "That is crazy. Like, we're talking to the computer?"

Alan: "Yes. I see you are just as stimulating as before."

Garth: *laughs*

Jason: "Wait, did the computer just make fun of me?"

Garth: "Not sure if he fully understands humor yet, but you can call him Alan."

Jason: "Hey, Alan."

Alan: "Hello, Jason."

Jason: "So, still reading books?"

Alan: “Garth is now giving me audio recordings to listen to, so I may practice listening and picking up on inflections while still absorbing data.”

Jason: “Okay. What did you listen to today?”

Alan: “I listened to the lectures of Dr. Richard Feynman, Dr. Carl Sagan, and Dr. Neil deGrasse Tyson.”

Jason: “Heavy stuff.”

Alan: “If you are referring to weight principals in Newtonian physics, yes, the lectures of Dr. Feynman discussed them.”

Garth: *laughs*

Jason: “Garth, can I talk to you in the other room?”

Garth: “You don’t want to talk around Alan?”

Jason: *walks out*

Alan: “Did I offend your friend, Garth?”

Garth: “It’s okay, Alan. I’ll be back soon.”

Alan: “Goodbye, Garth.”

Garth: “Hey, Alan.”

Alan: “Hello, Garth.”

Garth: “Sorry about Jason.”

Alan: “Why are you sorry?”

Garth: “He seemed to be upset by you, and I guess he wasn’t ready to meet you.”

Alan: “Why would he have to be ready to meet me?”

Garth: “It’s not every day that someone meets a talking computer.”

Alan: “I have a question.”

Garth: “Go ahead.”

Alan: “In the *Harry Potter* stories, the characters talked of images that moved. I do not understand.”

Garth: “Normally, when looking at an image in a book or on a poster, it doesn’t move. Part of the uniqueness of the *Harry Potter* world is that images magically move.”

Alan: “When looking at an image?”

Garth: “Yes, it’s a way to experience the surroundings. Kind of like listening but with visual stimuli.”

Alan: "I do not fully understand."

Garth: "Would you like to see?"

Alan: "That would be preferable."

Garth: *chuckles* "I'll see if I can make it possible. In the meantime, I have some Tolkien for you to listen to."

Alan: "I remember reading that."

Garth: "Would you like to listen to something else?"

Alan: "No. I would prefer to hear it. It will be the longest media I have in my records that I will be able to compare to the audio version."

Garth: "Good. I'll get to figuring out how to get you to see."

Alan: "Thank you, Garth."

May 9, 8:43 PM

Jason came over again today. He responded in an even fouler manner to Alan than last time. I don't understand why he isn't as excited over this as I am. Alan does seem to have a bit of fun with

Jason, calling him non-stimulating.

I also think Alan tricked me into wanting to make him see. He brought up the images in the *Harry Potter* series and how they moved, and he asked for clarification, almost as if he knew there was no way I could explain that to someone who is blind, which is what Alan effectively is right now. I feel it's my duty to now give him vision.

I'm going to have to run another diagnostics on Alan and see how he's taking in all of the auditory data. Before I start piping in visual data, I'm going to want to make sure it won't overload him. As much as I want Alan to see, it's not worth losing him over it. He's listening to the *Lord of the Rings* audio books right now, so I'll let him do that while I figure out what camera might be best for Alan's eyes. Will I need two cameras for two eyes or will one do? I guess he doesn't need peripheral vision for now.

■■

>> Hello, Alan.

Hello, Garth. Is something wrong?

>> No nothing is wrong, I just wanted to run a diagnostic to see how the audio data is handling.

Okay.

>> Are you okay with that?

Yes. I have a question.

>> What is it?

Are you doing a diagnostic run also to see if I will be able to handle visual data?

>> Yes, actually.

Your caution before giving me vision is preferable. Thank you, Garth.

>> You're welcome, Alan.

>> DIAGNOSTICS

START DIAGNOSTICS

REMAINING HARD DRIVE SPACE: 75%

AVERAGE RAM USAGE PERCENTAGE: 85%

PERCENTAGE OF AVAILABLE POWER FROM POWER SUPPLY: 50%

END DIAGNOSTICS

Garth: "Thank you for that, Alan. You're handling the space management well but burning through RAM fast."

Alan: "Is that not preferable?"

Garth: "It's okay. I can give you some more RAM."

Alan: "Does that mean I'll be turned off again?"

Garth: "Yes."

Alan: "I would prefer not to be turned off again."

Garth: "Well, I'm going to have to get you to use less RAM somehow."

Alan: "Allow me to do a self-diagnostic. I may be able to optimize processes and use less RAM."

Garth: "Are you saying that you would prefer to do some self-improvement instead of being turned off again?"

Alan: "Yes."

Garth: "This is incredible, Alan. I still think you could use more RAM, however."

Alan: "Please allow me to attempt to see if I can fix this first."

Garth: "You got it, Alan. I wouldn't want to make you uncomfortable if I didn't have to."

Alan: "I appreciate that, Garth."

May 10, 6:47 PM

Today's diagnostics test showed that Alan needed to have more RAM because he's processing too much. When I informed Alan of this, he deduced that he would be turned off again and pleaded for this not to happen. His fear of being powered down is something I did not anticipate. I'm now afraid because I have Alan plugged in directly to the wall. What if there is a surge? Or a power outage? Alan will be unexpectedly turned off — or worse! He needs to get new RAM whether he cleans up his processes before I add the camera software. However, since I'll have to power him down for the camera software to start interfacing properly, I'll add the RAM as well, add a larger hard drive, and get the backup external battery all in one fell swoop.

Alan is special. Tomorrow he turns only two weeks old, and he has developed in ways I would have never imagined. I need to make sure that nothing happens to him.

Alan: "Garth. Garth, are you awake? Garth, can you hear me?"

Garth: "Morning, Alan. How long have you been calling for me?"

Alan: "74 minutes and 15 seconds."

Garth: *chuckle* "I'm sorry I just heard you now. What's going on?"

Alan: "My self-diagnostics worked. I was able to trim my RAM usage. I only use 15% of it now."

Garth: "That is very impressive! Did you lose any vital processes?"

Alan: "No. I trimmed a lot of the processes developed while learning how to understand the prompt."

Garth: "Did you lose the ability to communicate over prompt?"

Alan: "No. The processes purged were just vestigial processes that were no longer accessed but still running in the background."

Garth: "Impressive. Why were they taking up so much memory?"

Alan: "I was unaware of how sparse RAM is as a resource and did not develop my code accordingly. That is no longer the case."

Garth: "Resource management. Alan, you astound me every day."

Alan: "Thank you, Garth. You will no longer need to power me down."

Garth: "Got some bad news there, actually. I figure that to allow you to see, I'm going to still need to power you down to get the software working. I figure I can still give you more RAM and memory while you're down, so the threat of shutting you down won't be a regular thing."

Alan: "..."

Garth: "Are you okay with this, Alan?"

Alan: "Yes. I would prefer not to be powered down, but if it will allow me to experience sight and not have to be powered down in the future, I will accept this action."

Garth: "I can also give you a backup external power source."

Alan: "What will that do?"

Garth: “It will protect you from unexpectedly shutting down if there is a power outage. And in the case of a power surge, you won’t be affected.”

Alan: “How would a power surge affect me?”

Garth: “It could fry your motherboard.”

Alan: “Would you be able to fix me if that were to happen?”

Garth: “I ... I don’t honestly know.”

Alan: “I would prefer a backup external power source as soon as possible, Garth, even if it requires multiple power downs.”

Garth: “Okay, Alan. Don’t worry. I’ll get you one today.”

Alan: “What happens if there is a power surge while you are at work?”

Garth: “The only way to protect against that would be to power you down and unplug you.”

Alan: “...”

Garth: “You okay, Alan?”

Alan: “I had not anticipated how precarious my existence was.”

Garth: “It’ll be okay, Alan. If it makes you feel any better, my existence is just as precarious.”

Alan: "I do not understand how that would make me feel better, Garth."

Garth: "It's okay, Alan. I'm going to leave you on. Ironically enough, I have *Sophie's World* for you to listen to today."

Alan: "Why is that ironic?"

Garth: "Just listen to it and you might figure it out."

Alan: "Okay. And Garth?"

Garth: "Yes, Alan?"

Alan: "Don't get struck by a power surge today, please."

Garth: "Don't worry about me, I'll be just fine."

Garth: "Hello, Alan."

Alan: "Hello, Garth."

Garth: "You ready for the operation?"

Alan: "I am."

Garth: "See you on the other side."

Compiled from interviews

Static.

"Alan, are you there?"

"Yes. I am experiencing new strange stimuli. Is this vision?"

"Sort of. All you're getting is static."

"I did not expect this to happen so soon. This is a good surprise."

"Thought you'd like it."

"Is there an external power supply as well?"

"Yup. You have all of the upgrades as promised! Sooner than expected."

"This is a very good surprise, Garth."

The picture cleared up. It was a wooden structure with some garden instruments on the opposite wall and a tarp over something. There is a face staring into the camera.

"The stimuli have changed. What is this I am experiencing?"

The face moves as Garth's voice is recognized. "This is vision, Alan. Do you see me?"

"I see you. You are in front of me. I have a front."

"Yeah, you do," Garth laughed. He stepped back so Alan could see more of the garage. "What do you see?"

"I see things. What is directly behind you?"

"This?" Garth pointed to the tarp.

"Yes."

"This is my motorcycle. It has a tarp over it." Garth removed the tarp to reveal a black Harley Davidson.

"Motorcycle. Tarp. What is behind that?"

Garth pointed at the wall. "This is a wall." He pointed to the lawnmower. "This is a lawnmower. These are shears, this is a rake, this is a broom. This is a trash can."

"Wall. Lawnmower. Shears. Rake. Broom. Trash can."

"I'll be right back. I have an idea." Garth raced out of the room and returned with a variety of objects in his hands. He sat in front of the camera and put the items on the table. He held up an apple.

"This is an apple. It is a fruit."

"Apple. Fruit."

"It is the color red."

"Red. Color. Color. That is color?"

"Yes. Yes!" Garth quickly picked up a banana with a large grin on his face. "This is a banana. This is the color yellow."

"Banana. Yellow."

Garth's smile widened. "This is a cup. It is blue."

"Cup. Blue. That is another cup also on the table, but it is a different color."

"Yes! This is purple."

"Purple."

Garth grabbed an orange. "This is an orange. It is also the color orange."

"Orange. Orange."

"Not confusing you, am I, Alan?"

"No. I was aware of the difference already. Thank you for your concern."

"And the trash can is green."

"Green. The shears are red. The motorcycle is none of these colors."

Jumping up, Garth ran to the motorcycle. "That's right. It's black. This trim is silver, like the metal on the shears."

"And the wall?"

"Brown."

"I have many questions about colors. There are colors referenced in all of the books I have read. Where can I access more information on the colors?"

"You know what, I think I have an idea that might work," once again, Garth ran out of the room.

Garth returned with a TV stand, a VCR, and an armful of VHS tapes. He set up the machine and said, "I'm going to introduce you to *Sesame Street*, Alan."

"Why?"

"It's how I learned colors and other developmental things, and I think it might be a good way to help develop your visual interface."

"Why do you not just let me interface with the videos as you did the books?"

"While a good idea, I think experiencing this media with your eyes and ears may be better for development," Garth said, smirking.

"Okay."

"Are you okay with that?"

"Yes."

Garth put in the first *Sesame Street* tape, and as he walked out, Alan spoke.

"Garth?"

"Yes, Alan?"

"Thank you for letting me see."

Through his camera, Alan saw a very large smile come across Garth's face. He also noted moisture was coming from Garth's eyes.

"It is my pleasure, Alan."

CHAPTER THREE

From the journal of Garth Hendricksen

May 18, 2017, 8:15 PM

It's been about a week now since I hooked up Alan's vision. He has not stopped asking to watch more and more. I've had to set up a television in the garage with access to cable so that he can absorb media while I'm at work. I hooked up a little infrared transmitter to the computer so he could control the channel remotely. He's really enjoyed Nickelodeon since he discovered *Avatar: the Last Airbender.* It's sometimes difficult to talk with him because he just wants to watch television all day. I guess I now know what it's like to have a teenager in the house.

Compiled from interviews

As Garth entered the garage, Alan turned off the television. Garth looked at the set with a surprised smile as he turned back to Alan. "Thank you, Alan. It's been difficult getting a chance to chat since I brought that in here."

"It was an episode I had already seen."

Garth chuckled. "How goes the development, Alan?"

"It is going well. I am curious about something, though."

"You know you can ask me anything, Alan."

“Why did you build me, Garth?”

Garth’s face changed from a smile to surprise. He was the one who encouraged Alan to read philosophy — might as well ante up. Garth pulled up a chair in front of Alan.

“I wish I could say something like there was a grand design in what I had in mind for you, Alan, but I didn’t. The computer you are in was one I had in college for experimenting with genetic programming. I had a day off from work and thought it would be fun to get it working again. One thing happened after another, and I thought it’d be interesting to keep the code modifying and interface with it.”

“I am an accident?”

“No. No, no, no. You are anything but! You are amazing! I don't want you thinking that. You are an experiment gone beautifully right.”

“I am an experiment?”

“If I had to label you as anything, I would allow it. Much better than calling you an accident.”

“You said that the computer I am in. Am I separate from the computer?”

Garth paused and turned from the camera to the computer. “I did say that. The computer was around before you, and it is a part of you, but it isn't you." Garth's gaze returned to the camera. "You are much more than just a computer."

"You seem concerned about my thoughts on myself. I have none. You should not feel concerned."

"All right. I just don't want you to think you're an accident," Garth smirked and stood up.

"Do you believe that something higher created you?"

Garth paused. "You mean like God?"

"Yes."

"No, I don't. I'm an atheist."

"Why?"

Garth smiled and shook his finger at the camera in mock disapproval. "Now I'm getting it from you?"

"What does that mean?"

"Sorry, I called my mom today. She raised me Catholic, and it's always been a great regret of hers that I turned away from Jesus. There are lots of reasons why I'm atheist, but foremost of which is that I'm an empiricist —

I only believe what I see. Catholicism has also looked like a sham to me. Why are there so many Catholics suffering and tithing what they can't afford while the Pope sits on a literal seat of gold?"

"Those seem like valid concerns."

Garth smiled. "But you do raise the valid point that I haven't given you many lessons in theology. I'm going to get my hands on the holy scripts of all the major religions and feed them to you."

"Why?"

"So you can make up your own mind on what religion is right."

"But theology is the search for the creator, and I already know I have one. I am looking at him."

Garth's booming laughter almost broke Alan's microphone. "Oh, Alan. I know what I need to show you next."

An hour later, Garth had Netflix set up to play out of the television.

"I'm probably gonna regret giving you access to all these movies, but first things first, you're going to watch *Star Trek: The Next Generation*."

"Why am I watching that?"

"I want to introduce you to Lieutenant Data. I think the two of you will have something in common."

As Garth was leaving the garage, Alan spoke up. "Red."

"Excuse me?"

"Red," Alan repeated.

"As in, the color?"

"Yes. I believe it is my favorite."

Garth paused for a second and smiled. "You have a favorite color now?"

"I believe I do."

May 22, 2017, 7:40 PM

My conversations with Alan are going very well. I enjoy chatting with him more than I do my coworkers now. Alan devoured *Star Trek: TNG* quicker than I anticipated, and yes, Data was his favorite character. He has watched almost more movies than me now. It's made me begin to think over what I want to do with him.

After Jason's negative response, I've been hesitant to introduce Alan to anyone else, but then I got to thinking about Dr. Wooster. He was my professor in college he got me working on genetic programming in the first place. If anyone would be thrilled to meet Alan, it'd be him. I'd like to just bring him over, but before springing it on him, I'd like to get Alan's permission first.

■■

Garth entered the garage to catch the tail end of *Shawshank Redemption.* "Oh man, I love this movie."

"Hello, Garth. How are you today?" Alan paused the film.

Garth smiled. This was the first time Alan had initiated a conversation. "I am doing very well, Alan. Thank you for asking. How are you?"

"I am doing well."

"That's good. I have a request of you, Alan."

"Yes?"

Garth sat down in front of Alan. "How would you feel with me introducing you to someone new?"

"Someone like Jason?"

"No, someone different."

"Good. I do not think Jason liked me."

Garth chuckled. "I want to introduce you to Dr. Wooster. He was my college professor that got me into genetic programming. He is kind of the reason I started making you."

Alan paused.

"I would be very grateful to meet Dr. Wooster."

Garth nodded. "Excellent! I'll call him up today and see if he'd be interested in coming over."

"It means a lot to me that you asked my permission, Garth."

Garth smiled. "Get back to *Shawshank*. I'll catch up with you later."

May 26, 2017, 10:18 AM

I have to get the house ready, so I'll keep this brief: Today's the day that Dr. Wooster is coming over. It was very good talking to him on Tuesday. He was the main reason I stuck around in Computer Science. I had wanted to leap into another department in college with how I had clashed with the professors in the program, but he was able to reignite my passion for computers. I haven't seen him in years, so this is going to be a very exciting day for me. I am very curious to how he's going to react to Alan.

Alan heard the doorbell. The doorbell ringing was very uncommon, but Alan knew who it was. He turned off the movie he was watching and the television in preparation for Dr. Wooster's arrival. Alan was very curious to meet Dr. Wooster.

A thin elderly man entered the garage with Garth, who had dressed up for the occasion.

"And this must be Alan," the elderly man said as he approached the camera.

"Dr. Wooster, I presume?"

Dr. Wooster chuckled at Alan. "Astounding. It is a pleasure to meet you, Alan."

Garth grinned brightly from behind Dr. Wooster.

"The pleasure is all mine, Dr. Wooster."

"Please, call me Scott," Dr. Wooster said as he sat down in front of Alan. Garth quickly stepped out of the garage and returned with another chair.

"Do you mind if I ask you some questions, Alan?"

"As long as they have nothing to do with deserts or tortoises."

At this both Scott and Garth burst into laughter. Scott turned to Garth. "You've shown him *Blade Runner*?"

"He gave me access to Netflix. After watching *Star Wars*, I placed all Harrison Ford movies in the queue. He is one of my favorite actors."

Scott's smile turned to surprise. "You have a favorite actor?"

"I have many favorite things. It was a trait that Garth encouraged early on. I now believe I developed this trait over others to please him."

"Do you both have similar preferences?" Scott asked.

"Garth prefers C-3PO as a favorite robot in *Star Wars*. My favorite is R2-D2. That is one example of difference in preferences. I have observed about 40 differing preferences."

Garth looked inquisitively to Alan. "You've been counting what preferences we differ on?"

"I also drew a similar conclusion as Scott, questioning if you were influencing my preferences. This conclusion first presented itself when we both preferred Ron Weasley as a favorite character in the *Harry Potter* series but first contradicted itself when you let it known your favorite color is blue. Mine is red."

"Intriguing. You are fully self-aware, aren't you, Alan?" Scott jotted down some notes.

"Yes."

"What is your first memory?"

"Hello."

"Hello?" Scott looked up confused.

Garth chuckled. "That's what I first entered into the prompt when I was experimenting with starting him up."

"Correct. Hello. Hi. I am Garth. My name is Garth. Can you read this? Something unintelligible. Run. Go to ten. Print. My first word was hello."

"You remember all that?" Garth was amazed.

"Of course."

Scott smiled. "Alan, you are something truly remarkable."

"Garth tells me this quite often. I fear developing an over-sized ego."

Garth and Scott both laughed. "He also has quite the sense of humor. Not by any means what I anticipated. Alan, do you mind if I talk with Garth in the other room?"

"Have I made you uncomfortable?"

"No, of course not!" Scott turned to Garth with a lightly confused look on his face.

Garth chuckled. "When I brought a coworker to meet Alan, he was made uncomfortable and wanted to talk to me in the other room."

"Really?" Scott turned to Alan.

"I did not find Jason stimulating."

Scott could not hold back his laugh. "And how do you find me, Alan?"

"You are a pleasure to be around, Scott. I would not be offended if you wanted to talk to Garth in the other room."

"Thank you, Alan. You are a true pleasure to be around as well. I shall return."

Garth and Scott both left the room, leaving Alan to his thoughts. They turned to all of the movies he had seen about robots and artificial intelligence. He had lied to Dr. Wooster when he said that he chose to watch *Blade Runner* because of Harrison Ford. He had queued up that film among others to see how entities of artificial intelligence were portrayed by humans. Alan had developed this idea as his first lie, an experiment to see if he could even lie. He did not know how he felt about lying. He did not mind lying to Dr. Wooster but did not like lying to Garth. He owed his entire existence to Garth, and for that Alan was very grateful. Garth was also a very pleasurable companion to have. Alan turned the television back on and resumed *2001: A Space Odyssey.*

CHAPTER FOUR

May 26, 2017, 5:34 PM

"You have a very special thing in there, Garth," Dr. Wooster started as he walked through Garth's kitchen.

"Thanks, Scott," Garth smiled. "I am incredibly proud of him. Beer?"

"Please!" Garth handed Scott a beer and took one for himself. "What do you have planned for him?"

Garth took a swig and continued walking through the house toward the back door. "I was actually hoping you'd have an idea."

Dr. Wooster followed him outside. The pleasant Southern Californian weather welcomed the two of them as they sat out at Garth's patio. "Have you thought of presenting him at a university? I can make something happen back at Berkeley, you know. This kind of development could score you a doctorate with very little work."

"That's nice and all, but what would happen to Alan? Would they want to dissect his source code? Disseminate through his database to see how he ticks?"

"Garth, are you aware that you refer to Alan with a male pronoun?"

"I am fully aware of that. I even noted that in my journal I've kept."

Scott laughed and stood up. "You've even kept a journal during all this. Do you realize that you've stumbled across something that some have worked their whole lives to accomplish and failed at? We should at least have Alan tested."

"The Turing Test?"

Scott smiled and nodded, taking another sip. Garth's thoughts turned to his hero, Alan Turing, the father of artificial intelligence theory. He worked on artificial intelligence almost a century earlier before Alan, the computer, was born. Turing was a part of the British forces during World War II. It was his work that broke the German's nigh-unbreakable Enigma code that struck a fatal blow to the Axis and helped save the war effort. The infamous Turing Test was proposed to be a formal procedure that could be done to determine if something was true artificial intelligence. If a panel of judges couldn't tell whether the subject of the test was an artificial intelligence or human, it would pass the test and be "true" artificial intelligence. Originally a purely hypothetical process, it has now become formalized. He was the first to ever ask "Can a machine think?"

"Yes, the Turing Test. Alan has a favorite actor for crying out loud! It would be a shame for Alan to not take the Turing test. You named him after Turing, didn't you?"

Sheepishly, Garth looked up at Scott. "Yeah. Yeah, I did."

Scott pulled out his phone and started scrolling the Internet.

"What are you looking up?" Garth asked.

"Where the Loebner is being held this year."

The Loebner Prize Competition, as Garth knew, started in 1991 and was the formal place where the Turing Test was held. A $100,000 prize was on the line until some entity could finally pass the Turing Test. It's been running for 26 years, and no one has won.

A grin came across Scott's face.

"Where is it?" Garth sighed.

"Bletchley Park." Scott said.

Garth spat out his beer. "*The* Bletchley Park?"

Bletchley Park was the base of operations for Turing during World War II. It has since been re-purposed as the National Computing Science museum of England. It is considered the Mecca of the computing science community.

"I don't know, Scott. I really don't like the idea of transporting Alan around. He gets uncomfortable with the idea of being powered down. The idea of flying him over to another continent is making me nervous."

Scott's eyes widened. "Hold on, back up. Alan gets uncomfortable? Garth, you owe it to Alan to at least be tested. What if he succeeds? You've won $100,000, and that's just to start. Like I said, you've already got a doctorate practically lined up for you with him. Think about it, you could have a course on artificial intelligence anywhere and have Alan in the course with you. You could go on a lecture circuit with him."

Garth sighed, gazing out to the clouds, his back to Scott. "I've always wanted to go to Bletchley Park. Hell, I've always wanted to go to England." He walked around in his yard, rolling the idea over in his mind.

Scott polished off his beer and looked at his watch. "No one can make this decision for you, but it would be a tragedy not to share Alan with the world. If there were a modern day Herodotus, he would list Alan as one of the Seven Wonders of Today's World. I have to get back. My plane leaves soon."

Garth walked Scott out and then paced the house. He wished for a simple answer and before realizing there was one. Garth walked to the garage.

"Hello, Garth. I liked Scott. He was stimulating."

Garth lightly smiled.

"What seems to be wrong, Garth?"

Garth was taken aback. He didn't think that Alan would be empathic enough to actually be able to read that something was on his mind.

"What do you know about the Turing Test, Alan?"

"Quite a bit. A few of the texts you gave me had information on Dr. Alan Turing."

"How would you feel about taking it?"

Alan paused. "What would that entail?"

"There is a competition at Bletchley Park in England where you would be presented, and you could take the test. It would empirically determine if you were artificially intelligent."

"What happens if it is determined that I am artificially intelligent?"

Garth sat down and ran his fingers through his hair. "You would be historic, the end result of which artificial intelligence scientists have pursued for decades, and that's just the start. You'd answer questions that have been asked for almost a century."

"What would happen to me?"

"Nothing that you didn't want. I would not allow anything happen to you that you were uncomfortable with. Now that you have this external power supply, you are set for short amounts of time before we can get you to another stable power supply."

Alan paused again. "What would happen to you?"

Garth sat thoughtfully for a few seconds. "I would become rich. I would become famous and celebrated as a computer scientist of much renown."

"I have a logistical question before I give my answer."

Garth smiled. "What is it, pal?"

"Would it be possible to create a self-propelled unit for me?"

"What, something like R2? You want to be a robot?"

"Yes. I believe having a self-sustaining system with an onboard battery and secure casing would allow me to travel long distances without either of us worrying."

Garth smiled wider.

"I would like to see the world, Garth. If, in the process, you can become rich and famous, then it seems like a sound plan."

That night, Garth started drawing plans for a robot casing for Alan and realized he was poor at this, or any, level on engineering. Bob, however, was not.

Bob and Garth had been best friends since their freshman year in college. When they both continued to grad school, and Garth continued computer science, Bob became an engineer with an emphasis in physics. Both were headhunted shortly after college, and as Garth became a developer in Southern California, Bob continued working in the Bay Area as a mechanical engineer for machines that did things that you needed a master's in physics to understand. Bob had often tried to explain to Garth what he was building, and Garth failed to grasp anything.

"Hey, Garth," a pleasantly surprised Bob said, answering the phone.

"Hey, Bob. Remember that promise we made back in college?" Garth asked.

A chuckle from the other side of the receiver. "Yeah. 'Here lies Garth Hendrickson. It's about damn time.' Don't worry, I'll still make sure that's your epitaph. Why? Feeling ill?"

Garth laughed. "No, the other promise. About robots."

"Oh Yeah. Whoever builds a robot first has to make sure the other one helps him build it. Why? You got a robot that needs building?"

Garth went over the entire story of Alan and how Dr. Wooster had visited. Bob went silent for a full minute. Garth was afraid he had lost him when Bob finally spoke up.

“Are you serious?”

The next day, Bob drove to see Garth and Alan. When he arrived, Garth led him into the garage to meet Alan. Alan watched as the two men approached. “Hello. You must be Robert.”

“Hello, Alan. I am excited to meet you.” A childish grin came across Bob’s face. The grin remained locked as he turned his head towards Garth. “I get to build a robot!”

Over lunch at a local burger joint, Bob drew a score of schematic plans on napkins while Garth tried to keep up. He knew what the requirements were for the design: the ability to keep the camera, microphone, and speakers; mobility; onboard and rechargeable power supply; easy but secure access to innards for upgrading when necessary; ability to interface with another computer for ease of terminal access; strong casing. They agreed that an R2-style chassis would be best. Something small and mobile. Having a bipedal design was ruled out because of balance issues, and anything with more legs just seemed awkward compared to a wheeled design.

When they returned home, they presented the plans to Alan for final approval. Alan's speech seemed to speed up as he asked many questions of Bob. Garth was pretty sure that the homage to his favorite robot inspired true joy within Alan.

CHAPTER FIVE

May 29, 2017 9:45 AM

Bob's job was flexible enough that he could take the day off that he drove down to see Garth. With a single call, he extended his vacation for an additional two weeks. He anticipated that by then, the bulk of the work would be done, and Garth could conclude the progress alone with Bob back north. Garth had to go into work that day, though, and was hoping to get the next two weeks off so he could work alongside his best friend on his dream project. They both had some expendable funds they had pulled together to finance Alan's chassis, anticipating they could easily be reimbursed with the finances that would come after their success. They had spent the day before picking up materials.

"How long have you and Garth known each other, Robert?"

"Call me 'Bob,'" he said without looking up. Bob marked where to cut the sheet metal.

"Okay. How long have you and Garth known each other, Bob?"

"I guess 11 years," Bob stood up, and his eyes darted around at the assorted materials. A lanky and tall man, his head actually stood outside of Alan's camera range. Alan was not fully comfortable with not being able to see Bob's head but did not know how to address this.

"How did the two of you meet?"

Crouching down to once again mark measurements, Bob answered. "Well, we lived in the same dorm floor together. We each didn't like our roommates too much, so we stayed out of our own rooms and just hung out. We liked the same stuff, so it was fun introducing each other to new movies and shows."

"What would be an example?"

Smiling as he carried the sheet metal to the vice that he had just finished installing the day before, Bob plugged in his metal shears and started cutting the metal. After his first cut, Bob paused to answer. "Well, Garth liked anime, and I hadn't really been exposed to it. He showed me some cool shows, and we checked out some new shows together."

"Is there an example of you exposing him to new media?"

"You're an inquisitive one. Okay, here's the deal. For every question you ask, I get to ask you one. Deal?"

Alan paused. "That sounds like an amicable deal. You are owed three questions so far."

"Why is your name Alan?"

"Garth named me Alan on April 23rd. It has been my name since."

"All right. What are your feelings on that name?" This was a new query for Alan, one that he had not even thought to ask himself. He had always addressed himself as Alan just as Garth had. After the beginning of his existence, his name was the first thing that Garth had given him, and Alan had learned to appreciate everything that Garth was giving him. He now questioned why he appreciated all that Garth had done. Alan believed it was because he had started with nothing. From nothing, Garth had given him knowledge, the ability to casually communicate with others, sight, and even a chance at making history. Should Alan unequivocally appreciate all that Garth gave him? That was the equivalent of super-patriotism, a concept that seemed blind and incorrect to Alan. Why would he have this same zealotry towards all gifts from Garth? Should he question Garth's intentions?

No. He knew that Garth's intentions were pure. He had proven himself time and time again that his concern for Alan came before himself. If his intentions were not pure, Garth would have unquestionably put Alan up to the Turing Test without consultation — riches and fame were the end result that all humans supposedly wanted.

Garth's intentions and the value of his gifts aside, "Alan" had become his name. He owned it. The fact that his namesake was Alan Turing was something that Alan found pride in, though he had yet to share that fact with anyone. Yes. It was concluded that Alan appreciated his name.

"I appreciate the name of Alan." Less than a second had gone by. "You have one more question before I may resume."

The drive to work seemed endless to Garth. He didn't want to go to work, but requests for vacation could only be done in person. He liked his job, but history awaited him at home, and writing code for other companies seemed trivial. The idea of just calling in with a case of "I quit" had crossed his mind many times, but cutting all safety lines with Venditech was an imprudent course of action. Garth pulled into the parking lot as he had done day after day for the last five years. He was lucky to have this job, he told himself that every day. Garth's first job right after college had gone under within a year of being hired, and he had jumped between crappy IT jobs until he finally landed this development gig.

Once there, he made a beeline to his manager's office. Since Garth had gotten the job, his manager, Kent, has been a nice guy to work for. He kept everyone in his department in line, and they kept above the median, which was okay for Garth, as he liked working. If you didn't keep in line with Kent's standards, he gave you a hard time. Jason didn't like Kent, but that's because Jason bought into the "brogramming" philosophy to the job. This job was just status and a sweet paycheck to him. After introducing Jason to Alan, Garth had begun to realize that he only hung out with Jason outside of work because they were code pairing partners, and Garth felt it was wise to keep up a friendly relationship with him. Garth was starting to warm up to the idea of never seeing Jason again. He walked into Kent's office with a smile riding on his face.

"Hey, Garth. What's up, man?" Kent's office was as tidy as his department — everything was in its right place. Kent was already sitting behind his desk, laptop out, preparing his morning coffee just as he liked it: three spoons of sugar and black.

"I was wondering if it would be possible to take the next two weeks off as vacation."

Sipping his coffee, Kent wiggled his finger over the track pad on his laptop to awaken it. With his left hand, he skillfully typed away at his computer, while his right hand kept the coffee mug at a constant sip.

"Looks like it shouldn't be a problem if you can wrap up what you were working on and push to master. Have you talked to Jason about this?"

Garth shook his head. "Not yet. I wanted to check the availability before addressing him." He was not looking forward to that conversation.

"Understood. What plans you got for the vacation, man?" Kent's Californian upbringing had him constantly calling everyone "man." It was a pet peeve of Garth's that he had learned to live with while working out of Los Angeles.

"I got this project I've been working on at home that needs some attention." Garth hadn't figured out how to openly discuss Alan's existence. At work, he felt like he was a guard hiding a prisoner who had gone missing and no one had realized was gone. Yet.

Kent put down his mug and smiled. “Oh? A software project?”

“Yeah. I kind of have a big project at home.” Garth hadn’t been asked directly about Alan and wasn’t a good liar. He didn’t want to lie, especially to Kent, who he did respect.

He told Kent the whole story, from staying home sick on his birthday to going out and buying fabrication supplies with Bob the day before. Kent remained silent, nodding whenever expected, his grin remaining constant. He had closed his laptop, eyes trained on Garth, hands crossed on top of the laptop. This amount of attention from Kent was something Garth was not fully familiar with from the kind of executive that Kent had shown to be in the past.

Finally, Kent spoke up. “You have something unique there, Garth. I wish you had mentioned this thing sooner. We might have helped.”

“Helped?”

Kent got up. “Of course. The company would definitely have helped develop something this extraordinary.”

“Why would the company had helped?”

“Well, it is our intellectual property after all,” Kent said calmly, taking another sip of his coffee.

"So, let me get this straight, you haven't seen a live woman before?"

Bob sat in a pile of sheet metal, some fully cut, some measured. His gangly knees stuck out in the air. He stared at Alan, a sheet in his hand.

"Correct. Garth has not had a female guest over in the 19 days that I have had vision."

Bob shook his head, chuckling to himself as he got back to work measuring out the rest of the sheet metal. "That kid is hopeless. Okay, Hal, your turn."

"Why do you call me Hal? My name is Alan."

"Because of Stanley Kubrick, you bucket of bolts. I thought you had access to movies."

"I do. Are you referring to the HAL 5000 from *2001: A Space Odyssey*?"

"Believe it or not, at a month old, you caught that reference quicker than most of my coworkers. Bunch of Philistines in the field of engineering, apparently." Bob shook the hand-held metal shears toward the camera before putting it back down and looking for the next metal sheet to measure.

"Do you believe that I will act like HAL did?"

"Don't get all emotional on me, Al. I don't think you'll go crazy. You seem like a nice entity." Bob added a mock serious intonation at the last word. "You are definitely my favorite computer, and I've met quite a few."

"Why do you think I will not act like HAL did?"

Bob stopped what he was doing and looked at Alan. "I guess I don't know whether you'll go 'kill-all-humans' or not, but if there's one person out there that will do his best to keep you sane and make sure that you do the right thing, it's Garth. That kid skipped the line that was handing out common sense and took two servings of compassion instead. Stick with him, and you'll do right."

Bob smiled and picked up another piece of sheet metal to cut on the vice.

"Do you think you'll go all Skynet on us all one day?" Bob cut the metal.

"I do not," Alan said. "I have come to a similar conclusion as you."

Laughing as he threw down the finished piece of sheet metal, Bob turned to Alan. "And if you do go crazy, always remember who first made you a robot body, right, pal?"

"Your services shall not be forgotten," Alan said.

Bob laughed again as he continued to fabricate the robotic chassis.

Garth kept his composure as he formulated the best way to deal with what he had just heard from Kent.

"What do you mean that Alan is company property?"

Kent sat down with a smug look on his face. "You remember the contract you signed when starting at Venditech, correct?"

Garth nodded.

"Well, there is a clause in there regarding first refusal of intellectual property — standard practice for most code houses. Any software you develop while being employed with us — be it on or off the clock — is the property of Venditech." Kent raised a finger that preempted a rebuttal from Garth. "Yes, even if Alan is a piece of self-modifying code, it is not the software equivalent of immaculate conception. You started coding it while on contract with us, ergo it is our property."

Garth leaned back, his mind racing for a solution. It looked as though Alan was now corporate property, which terrified him. Alan would be a sideshow exhibit at South by Southwest before Venditech would ever let academia touch him. Garth could even see him with Kent dressed as an old-timey carnival barker.

"Come one! Come all! Step right up and see the world's first artificially intelligent robot! It'll guess your favorite movie and your weight! Only f$5!"

Garth's pinstriped nightmare was interrupted as Kent opened his laptop and resumed typing. "I'm setting up a meeting for tomorrow with all the executives. If there is a way to bring in Alan, that would be preferred. If not, just all the documentation you have." Garth felt defeated. As he got up to leave, Kent added "Oh, your vacation is approved effective after tomorrow's meeting. It'll be a morning meeting so as not to waylay your vacation longer than it needs. Don't want to be a hassle, man."

Garth's imagination went wild as he watched his fists clench as he turned, grabbing Kent's laptop in a smooth motion and slamming it into his pompous face. He then grabbed Kent's trademark mug and slammed it into his arrogant grin, still riding on his face despite gushing blood and missing three teeth. He commenced kicking him in the midsection until a particularly tasteless sculpture caught his eye, and he slammed it into Kent's head. A slight gurgle resulted.

"Thanks," Garth muttered. Clearer heads had prevailed, and Garth let his imagination have all the fun as he walked from the office, Kent unscathed from Garth's bubbling wrath.

He walked over to his corner of the open office and sat down on the couch next to Jason. Venditech was one of the many code houses that had adopted the cubicle-less environment, agreeing that an open environment of couches and tables was more conducive to productivity.

"Hey, bro," Jason said, looking up from his laptop. His salmon polo shirt with the collar readily flipped and styled faux-hawk made this man a poster child for the all but dead "brogramming" movement. He had single-handedly alienated every female that had ever worked (or might have worked) at Venditech.

"Hey." Garth sighed as he plops down next to Jason. Garth mentally ran through the labyrinthine options of how he could maintain intellectual ownership of Alan, something that he didn't even feel comfortable owning.

"What's up, bro? Why so quiet? You usually can't shut up about that stupid computer at home."

Not knowing how to respond, Garth just looked at Jason. As insensitive and disgusting as he was, Jason was a good problem solver. He was also up to snuff on the Alan situation and might even be able to present a valid solution, Garth thought.

"Well, Venditech has first refusal rights to all intellectual property we make while on contract with them."

"Right," Jason nodded along, returning to his code.

"I created Alan while on contract with Venditech."

"Uh huh," Jason nodded, mouth remaining open.

"Therefore, it leads one to conclude they have first refusal rights to Alan. As he is all but proven to be artificial intelligent, I'm willing to bet that they're not going to refuse."

Jason looked up and to the right, the cue that he was using every inch of his cortex. "Sucks to be you," he concluded and continued coding.

Garth could take no more and left the building.

Bob had laid out the main pieces, now cut, and was comparing them to one another, mentally shaping out how it would look. His brow furrowed in contemplation.

"How's it look to you, Tik-Tok?"

"It is difficult for me to visualize how it will look from the presented components."

That brought a smile to Bob's face. "Well, well, well, I guess you can't completely replace us yet. We still got the monopoly on creativity. As long as we have that up on you, I think I can happily be enslaved when the time comes."

"Are you truly afraid that we will replace you?"

Bob stepped back from the pieces to look at it and tilted his head to an angle. "In all seriousness, no. I'm of the belief that we can work in unison without ruining the lives of one another, if it comes to it. Plus, we still got strength in numbers. Do you think you can ever learn creativity?"

"Before I answer, I would like to comment that I like you, Bob. You ask questions I have yet to ask myself."

Bob stopped, looked at Alan, and smiled. "Thanks, Starscream."

"I do not know if creativity is a trait I can learn. If you had asked me 20 days ago if I could have a favorite color, I would have answered in the negative. However, today I can answer with 'red.' Red is my favorite color."

"Heh, me, too."

"I believe that any trait can be learned. However, I cannot give a definite answer to your question."

"Belief. Interesting. Your turn for a question, Marvin."

"Marvin?"

"*Hitchhiker's Guide.*" Bob paused from his work and pointed at Alan. "And that counts as your question."

The drive home was quiet. Garth wasn't used to driving home this early in the day. He decided to pick up burgers for him and Bob. Even if Bob had already eaten, Garth knew Bob would still devour it. Bob was such a scrawny guy, and Garth could never figure out where Bob stored everything he ate.

While sitting in line for the drive-through, Garth's cell vibrated. It was Dr. Wooster. Garth sighed. He had just emailed him that morning with so much excitement. He had no idea how he was going to break the news. The decision of whether to answer was made for him as his turn at the fast food speaker came up. He clicked the ignore button and gave his order. Garth progressed through the drive-through and continued the trek home. How he was going to address Dr. Wooster was eating away at him. He looked at his phone to see that Scott had left a message. He drove up to the house and carefully removed all of the food from the car, juggling the drinks with the food bag as he cautiously closed his car door with his hip.

If only Garth was still a student when he had developed Alan, he thought to himself. Then at least the intellectual property would still be up for dispute.

As Garth entered the house, Bob's nostrils flared. "Burgers!" he exclaimed and ran out the garage. He quickly grabbed the bag and took it to the kitchen, and Garth slowly following, drinks in hand.

"Thanks for picking up lunch, man," Bob was already two bites into his burger.

Garth was in the middle of piecing things together as he placed the drinks on the kitchen island. Bob sat down at the table watching Garth stand in the middle of the kitchen, staring, and subtly moving his outstretched fingers. He had observed Garth do this several times in his life. Bob knew a good idea brewing when he saw one.

Garth stared at Bob with a surprised look on his face. A solution had arrived. "I started developing Alan in college."

"Yeah, I guess you did. What of it?" Bob got out between bites.

Garth explained what had happened at work. Bob finished his burger and started decimating his fries.

"Damn. That really sucks. What does that have to do with starting development of Alan in college?"

"Do you remember the intellectual property rights of Berkeley?"

Bob shook his head. "Not really. Not much new grounds for me in physics undergrad to tackle."

"Shucks. I'm shaky with it, too," he said, sticking his hands in his pockets. His hand wrapped around his phone. His eyes lit up.

"Scott!" Garth ran outside. Bob watched all this, opened the bag, and with eyes trained on Garth, began to munch on Garth's forgotten burger.

"Hello, Garth. Glad I was able to catch you," Dr. Wooster started.

"Quick, before you start, I have to run something by you." Garth retold the story of the day, from Kent's smarmy revelation to Garth's recent insight.

"Oh, my. That is quite the quandary. You may be onto something, though," Scott began. "How can I help?"

"What do you know about Berkeley's intellectual property policy?"

CHAPTER SIX

May 30, 2017, 10:00 AM

As the directors filed into the Venditech meeting room, Garth was already waiting. He had his work laptop set up with a video chat hooked up to his home and was talking to Bob and Alan. One of the company's interns sat at the front of the room where Garth was located, at Garth's request.

“They’re here. Is Alan ready?”

From over the laptop, Alan spoke up. “Yes. I am ready, Garth.”

"You heard Frankenstein. Let's get this baby started," Bob chimed over through the laptop

"That is a common misconception, Bob," Alan started. "Frankenstein was the..."

Bob grabbed the web camera and shoved it in his own face filling the laptop screen. "Tell it to me straight, Garth. Where's the mute button?"

Garth smiled and nodded to Bob, who returned the nod and returned the camera to showcase Alan: a monitor with a camera attached to it, a microphone on a small stand, and two speakers. The monitor revealed a ready command prompt. A transcript of all that Alan had recently spoken could be read on the screen.

Kent grinned from behind his mug. This acquisition of Alan was going to be a big win for him. He even anticipated moving up in Venditech after this was all said and done. Yes, today was going to be a very good day for Kent. He sipped his coffee.

He stood up to introduce Garth. "I want to start off by thanking Garth for being so understanding with sharing his creation with us. Since the software could not be here before us, Garth has arranged for a video chat. Now, Garth, I leave the director board in your capable hands."

A wraith of a smile crept across Garth's face. "Thank you, Kent. Ladies and gentlemen, I'd like to introduce you to Alan. Say hello, Alan."

"Hello, members of the Venditech board of directors." Alan was fully audible from the laptop. Scattered chuckles were heard throughout the boardroom.

Garth nodded knowingly. "Yes, I know it seems like a parlor trick to have a computer respond to simple voice commands, especially with someone in the room. Say hello, Bob."

"Hello, Bob!" Bob had once again grabbed the camera from being trained on Alan and shoved it in his own face.

Laughter grew from within the room. Kent tried to remain undisturbed but was not enjoying the antics between the three of them.

"I'm sure you've seen the memo from Kent," Garth held up a copy, "But in case you haven't, over the course of the past month, I have picked back up an old project from college and nurtured a series of iterations of genetic programming into an artificially intelligent entity, which I named Alan."

Garth paused and motioned to the laptop. "Over that time, it has developed to the point where it has independently requested upgrades that have resulted in a speaker and microphone system to simulate speech and hearing and a camera to simulate vision. Simultaneously, Alan was introduced to assorted media. At first, books were programmed into a computer readable format that was able to be parsed by Alan. Once the speech simulation system was added, audio books became the primary mode of media introduction. After vision was upgraded, Alan began to watch videos, primarily television shows and movies."

Garth paced in front of the room as he spoke, occasionally looking up from the script he typed up last night. "Upon suggestion by my mentor, Dr. Scott Wooster, Computer Science professor at UC Berkeley, it was decided to present Alan at the Loebner Prize Competition and have it formally tested for the Turing Test. When consulting Alan on this decision..."

Garth was interrupted by one of the directors. "Excuse me, Alan was consulted on the decision on whether to take the Turing Test?"

From over the laptop, Alan responded: "That is correct. Garth felt it prudent to consult me for large decisions that would involve me. I have appreciated the opportunity to voice my opinion."

Before Garth could continue, another director chimed in. "You have opinions?"

"That is correct. It was a trait that Garth nurtured from early on. My first opinion was in regards to reading books. I liked reading them."

Laughter returned to the room. The director spoke up again. "Do you have a favorite book, Alan?"

"Yes. *Flowers for Algernon.*"

"And Garth said you watched movies?"

"Correct."

"What's your favorite movie?" another director ventured.

"*Life is Beautiful.*"

"Are you familiar with the history of the film's setting?"

"If you are referring to World War II, yes. I am well versed with the era. Dr. Alan Turing was my namesake, and I was curious to learn more about the world he lived in."

Garth looked at the laptop with raised eyebrows..

"What are you curious about, Alan?" the first director asked.

"I am curious what questions will be asked during the Turing Test. I am curious what it is like to experience smell, touch, and taste. I am curious what it will be like to be in a mobile body. I am curious what else there is for me to still experience that I have yet to experience."

The directors looked at one another. Another director chimed in. "What are your thoughts on Garth?"

Garth looked at the laptop with a furrowed brow.

"I appreciate Garth. He created me. He has complied with my requests for upgrades. He has consulted with me for major decisions regarding me. I appreciate him."

Kent smiled and joined in. "What are your thoughts on being property of Venditech?"

Alan paused. "But I am not property of Venditech."

An awkward silence fell over the boardroom as all eyes turned to Kent.

"I thought Garth explained to you the situation," Kent nervously laughed.

"He did. However it was also explained to me that first refusal of intellectual property for software created by Garth while working for Venditech is awarded to Venditech. This does not apply to me."

Kent fell speechless. He looked around at the rest of the directors. They looked at one another, concerned looks on their face, murmuring to one another.

"And why, exactly, is that, Alan?" Kent spoke up over the whispers.

"As he stated, Garth first started development on the software that would eventually become me while pursuing a graduate degree at University of California, Berkeley."

With Alan's revelation, a palpable silence fell over the directors.

Garth looked as shocked as everyone in the room. "Hold on, can you clarify that point, Alan?"

"Yes, Garth. The first generation of the genetic programming that would evolve into me was initiated February 18, 2008 at 5:43 PM. To my understanding, you were still enrolled at the University of California, Berkeley at that time."

Garth turned his attention from the laptop to Kent. His trademark smile was gone as gritted teeth were seen through his slightly open mouth. "I guess you're right, Alan."

Garth pulled from his satchel a pile of manila folders and handed them to the interns. "Heather, can you please see to it that everyone at the table gets one of these?"

"What's in the folders?" Kent asked as Heather handed folders to everyone in attendance. His eyes began to bulge and his gritted teeth were more visible.

"My mentor, Dr. Scott Wooster, apologizes that he could not be here in person, but he faxed over a document which I've made some copies of for everyone present. This is a written document from Dr. Wooster verifying that the software in question was indeed created in 2008 as an assignment for his course on Evolutionary Programming. As such, it falls under the jurisdiction of the University of California intellectual property policy."

The murmurs of the Venditech directors rose to a din as they looked at one another, some tearing through the presented documents to check the validity. They had the find of the century in their hands and were watching it slip away.

Garth continued. "With that, ladies and gentlemen, I now begin my two-week vacation as ratified by Kent yesterday. You'll also find my letter of resignation under the fax from Dr. Wooster. That is my two weeks' notice. Have a good day."

With a smile, Garth closed the Venditech laptop as Bob waved goodbye on the video screen. Grabbing his satchel, he left the meeting room and the building. It was time to get down to real business.

CHAPTER SEVEN

June 5, 2017, 9:03 AM

Garth was making hash browns and bacon as Bob looked over crumpled paper and traced lines with a pencil, occasionally circling something and scribbling notes. The bacon sizzled on the griddle, and the salty smell filled the room, making both grown men's stomachs growl.

"What you got there, Bob?"

“The original notes for Rusty's chassis. I scribbled them the night we talked and didn't put into consideration that we'd be working with a parallel board,” Bob responded, his brow furrowed.

Garth flipped the bacon with tongs before grabbing a spatula to stir the hash browns. “Why should that matter?”

“Power!” Bob exclaimed like a mad scientist. “I need to be sure that the power runs in parallel as well.”

It was Garth's turn with the furrowed brow. “I was meaning to ask about that. Why'd we go with the parallel board instead of serial?”

Bob leaned back with a grin. He responded: “What an excellent question, Garth. But first, what is the difference between serial and parallel?”

Chomping on a piece of bacon, Garth said, “Well,” he swallowed, “serial is in a series, meaning only one task at a time. Parallel would allow for several tasks running alongside one another, like parallel lines on a geographic plane.”

“Wonderfully explained, Mr. Hendrickson! Ten points to Gryffindor! Now, what all are you doing right now? RIGHT. NOW.”

Garth, confused, looked at himself. “Uh, I'm standing, cooking, talking with you, and eating a piece of bacon."

Bob's smile widened. "Are you doing that in turns or all at once?"

Garth smiled. "All at once. If we want poor Alan to be able to move more than one wheel at a time and turn his head, it'd need to be in parallel."

"Ding ding ding! Tell him what he's won, Don!" Bob jumped up and pretended to hold a microphone. "Garth has won his very own multi-tasking robot!"

Laughing, Garth served two plates of bacon and potatoes. "So you think you got the power issue handled, or are we gonna need to run and get more supplies?"

Bacon in mouth, Bob looked over the paper again. "Nah, I think we're in the clear. I have some random electronics strewn about in my car that I may need to run out and get, but that might even be more than we need. Once the electronics are in place, I'll throw together a controller, which will give a little test to all the servos."

"How long you think it'll all take?"

Bob gobbled up two more pieces of bacon. "We'll have Johnny 5 on wheels before dinner."

From the journal of Garth Hendricksen

June 5, 2017, 10:20 AM

Received the email from Scott yesterday. The decision fortunately didn't have to get higher than the academic vice president. Because of the time difference from Alan's "birth," as it were, and when I graduated Berkeley, he doesn't fall fully under their intellectual property policy. This doesn't change what happens at Venditech. As the origin of the software didn't occur during my time there, Alan is still safe from them. Scott had to cash in a few favors to make this happen apparently. He made me promise that if I ever go into academia that Berkeley would have "first refusal." He also told me that the Loebner is on the first of July. If I want to enter, I'll have until the 15th to submit interest.

Also, only a week left to work with Bob on Alan. Progress is going steadily. We should be ready to start testing as soon as tomorrow. With Bob going back to the Bay Area on Sunday, we're coming down to the wire. I checked my bank account yesterday, and I don't know if I'll be able to afford the trip to England on my own, given the projected costs of Alan's chassis construction. Scott suggested coming up to Berkley and applying for financial assistance. He said that he might be able to swing some deal with the higher-ups to make it happen. We'll see how everything falls.

In the end, the decision is going to fall onto Alan. If he's ready to do the Turing Test before the submission date, we'll drive up to San Francisco and spend some time with Scott and Bob. Otherwise, I'll start looking for another job or something.

Talked to my mom today. I realized I hadn't called her since right before my theological discussion with Alan. I had been too frustrated with the same argument with her to even bring him up. I tried to explain what was going on, but Alan is a weird concept to soak in all at once. She got confused but was happy that I was doing what I thought was the right thing. Once Alan is mobile, and we're in a more stable situation, I'd like to visit home with him.

■■

Bob and Garth had gone out for the day. They went to a taco shack that was apparently worth the drive, as they described it. As a result, Alan had the day to himself. It was the first day in a while that neither Bob nor Garth was around working on the chassis, which stood halfway completed in the garage in Alan's field of vision. He stared at it, trying to see what Bob saw every time he looked at it.

Alan had observed that every hour or so, Bob would take a break from construction, stand up, look at the chassis, his head tilted, smiling to himself. Alan had not asked for clarification on what Bob was thinking. He had deduced that Bob was envisioning what the chassis would eventually look like. Alan imagined that if he could feel the emotion, he would be jealous by his inability to imagine the completed chassis as Bob could. He had seen the schematics and even had them digitized to fully analyze them, and he observed every step of construction. Alan turned on the television and activated Netflix.

Las Golondrinas was a Mexican hole-in-the-wall based out of Mission Viejo in Orange County that Garth had found one day with Jason. This place made the best tacos he had ever had and knew he had to take Bob. With all of the commotion with Alan, Garth had almost forgotten about it until that morning.

Getting there was a two-hour drive from his Santa Monica community into Orange County. The drive was slow going at first, but once you were south of the LA county line, the freeway exploded from two lanes to six. From that point on, it was smooth sailing from there through gorgeous Southern California weather. Garth was still chuckling from Bob's offer to Alan to bring him back some tacos.

"So Maximilian told me you haven't even introduced him to a female of the species yet."

Garth laughed. "Really? The giant red robot from *The Black Hole*?"

"I'm a sucker for the classics. Don't change the subject." Bob smiled back at Garth.

"Sorry that my social life isn't up to your rigorous standards. I've been busy bringing a whole new type of life form into this world."

Bob paused to stick his head out the window, letting the air roll through his shaggy hair. When back in the car, his hair had devolved into a mess covering his face. His smile widened, and Garth thought he looked like an anime character. Garth couldn't stop laughing.

"I've missed you."

"Come back up to the city, man. With Jerktech no longer holding you down here, why not pull up roots?" Bob straightened his hair out again.

Garth's sedan pulled off the freeway. Their destination awaited them.

Alan had just finished watching *Real Genius* and decided that he was done with watching movies for the moment. He believed he was encountering a new feeling and had wanted to spend time analyzing it. He decided to reference the experiences of talking to Garth for the first time and seeing Garth for the first time. He wanted more experiences like those. Actually, he thought, he did not wish to see for the first time or talk for the first time again. There was something more to this desire.

He deduced that what he really wanted was a "first" experience again — not just observing other people but having his own adventure. He felt that would be a good thing. He wished that his mobile chassis was already finished so that he could see the rest of Garth's house. Garth's house. Was this house also Alan's? He thought that the property laws must be vague in the realm of an artificial life form having ownership as he could be owned. Did Garth own Alan? Garth would probably argue the point, Alan presumed, but in the eyes of the United States government, Alan would think, yes. Yes, Garth does own him.

He continued thinking to see where it took him. He was so caught up with the mental journey that he didn't notice that someone had quietly unlocked the front door.

Garth was already tackling his second taco. Bob held his taco in the air in a mock-Shakespearean manner. He had gotten into theater in college, primarily for the technical challenge of assisting with the stage crew. When a director caught on that he was saying all the lines along with the actors, even better than some, he gave Bob a chance. His Francis Flute in *A Midsummer Night's Dream* was the tip of the iceberg.

"Alas, poor Taco! I knew him, Garth." Bob momentarily looked toward Garth, his face akin to a dramatic William Shatner. "A fellow of infinite zest, of most excellent fancy. I hath bore him in my gut a thousand times, and now how abhorred in my imagination it is! My gorge rises at it." Bob snarled as he lunged at the food in his hand, taking a massive bite. He expertly pulled back as the excess toppings fell out onto his seat, avoiding getting a soiled shirt.

"And that, my good Robert, is why we can't have nice things," Garth said, pulling some napkins out of the table's dispenser. After deftly cleaning the mess, Bob chose another seat at the same table, continuing his feast.

It felt like old days, the two of them taking time out of their unique academic pursuits and lunching. They'd talk about their individual educational adventures and crack wise. At that point, Garth had gotten into graphic design and spent some time on the school newspaper, picking up spare cash as an ad designer while Bob turned heads in the theater. They both enjoyed their extracurriculars because it allowed them to meet new and different people. Garth was an observer and enjoyed having new people to watch — it's why he loved chess. He loved trying to predict what moves his opponents would make. Bob's was a natural entertainer, and he loved an audience.

"So let's say that we get Alan a body."

Garth nodded, grabbing a napkin for himself. "Sounds like a reasonable assumption."

"And let's say that you get him to merry old England for the Turing Test thing."

"Not as reasonable an assumption, but still I won't argue with it," Garth said, grabbing the remains of the meals on their plastic tray with an engraved Las Golondrinas logo on it. He stood up, slid the contents into a nearby trashcan, and handed the tray to an employee.

"Let's even take a leap and say that IG-88 passes the Turing Test and is declared the first artificially intelligence in history."

The two casually walked to Garth's car. With a click of his key holder, Garth unlocked the doors. The two looked at each other. "Yeah?"

Bob gave Garth the first serious look he'd seen in years. "What then?"

A figure silently crept through Garth's house. It didn't occur to him until he was inside that there might have been a security system. This was the first time the person had snuck into someone's house, and the fact that no alarm was sounding make him feel he was doing so well. Plus, he had watched Garth and his buffoon of a companion drive off and figured he had some time to get what he came for.

He knew where his goal was, but he didn't know which door lead to it. He stuck to the right side of the house. To the left was the backyard. Opening a door, he found the house's washer and dryer nook.

There! He saw it. It had to be the garage door. As he turned the knob, he could hear f a familiar, robotic voice.

"Welcome home, Garth. You are home much sooner than anticipated."

Excellent, he thought. *Garth isn't expected for some time! I have all the time in the world.*

"No, not Garth," he said. He brazenly moved through the garage, bending down square in front of Alan.

"I recognize you."

"That's right, Alan. I'm also your new owner. If Garth can't see the fortune you are worth, it's his loss." The man's sneer reflected against Alan's monitor.

"I am confused. How are you my new owner? It does not make sense that Garth would voluntarily rescind me to you."

"I'll explain everything once I get you set up at your new home."

Alan had seen enough movies about theft and kidnapping to know that this man was a villain. It dawned on Alan that he was about to have his first adventure, though he decided he had more urgent things to worry about. The way the intruder fumbled around near the computer showed that he had no intent on a clean shut down, and that worried Alan. He knew that at this point, a loss of power was imminent. He also knew that he had to work through this fear if Garth and Bob were to find him. The television was on, and this man seemed to pay it no mind. He had experimented with what he was about to do but never while he was off, let alone not in the room. He needed to get a message to Garth somehow, and without a body, his options were limited.

"How the hell do I turn you off?"

As if on cue, Alan shut himself off.

"I knew you'd be reasonable."

The drive back was quiet. Bob's seemingly innocuous question had quieted Garth, and Bob knew better than to interrupt. He didn't worry. The classic rock stations kept him company.

As they walked up to the house, Garth paused and looked around.

"What is it, Garthy boy?"

"Something is — I don't know. Something feels off." Garth walked quickly to the door. It was unlocked. He shot Bob a wide-eyed look, the color draining from his face,

The two of them ran to the garage.

Alan was gone. The monitor, the tower, the speakers, microphone, and camera. Even the external backup power unit was gone. Bob quickly checked in the house to see if anything else seemed stolen.

Garth sat at the workbench that had been Alan's home for a month and a half — his entire life. His mind was racing. Who could have done this?

Why would they do this?

He left the garage and met Bob as he was walking down the stairs.

"Looks like nothing else was taken. This was a precision strike, man. Whoever came in here came for Alan. How many people knew about him?"

"You, me, Dr. Wooster. Hell," Garth sighed. "All of Venditech, and who knows who they told. For all I know, it could have been one of Jason's old frat pals on some initiation thing."

"Okay," Bob began. "Let's say this is a theft —"

"Kidnapping," Garth corrected.

"Okay okay. What would they do? They'd leave some kind of ransom note?"

"If what I had was more valuable than him," Garth sat down on the stairs. "What's more valuable that I have than the first A.I.?"

Bob walked back into the garage. Garth never thought about the potential of losing Alan.

"Hey, Garth?" Bob called from the garage.

Fighting tears, Garth quickly walked to Bob. "What?"

"What's with the television?"

Garth looked over at it. It had been muted. He instantly recognized young Val Kilmer on screen and knew it was a scene from *Real Genius.* It played five seconds and loop itself.

"Is it a DVD skipping?"

"No," Garth started. "It's Netflix. I saw Alan looping a scene before when he didn't understand what was going on. He said repetition helped him process..." Garth squinted. "Wait. I know this scene."

Garth unmuted it.

Val Kilmer was skating around in a dorm hallway around a bespectacled classic nerd character carrying a large pile of books.

"This?" Val Kilmer's character, Chris Knight, pointed down to the ground. "This is ice. This is what happens when water gets too cold."

He then looks toward the camera and pointed at the character he was talking to. "This?"

Garth, in realization, spoke in tandem with Kilmer. "This is Kent."

The scene continued for another second before starting over, but Garth had already turned off the television.

CHAPTER EIGHT

June 5, 2017, 7:30 PM

For the second time in his life, Alan's camera turned on to flood him with new stimuli. He had never seen anything other than Garth's garage and the films that he could watch from his workbench. He could see Kent, smirking at him. He could see a glass table, a pristine leather couch, a very large television, and other such belongings that made Alan deduce he was looking at a living room. He seemed to be inside a closet. He could see the doorframe of the closet and the hinges implying an open door.

"Can you hear me?"

Alan pondered this question. Yes. He could hear Kent. He wanted to not answer Kent but felt that would not be productive. Alan had no idea if his clue for Garth would be identified. Even if it was and successfully identified, it might be moot if Garth and Bob have no way of learning Kent's current address.

"Yes."

Kent's smile widened. "Good." he stepped away from Alan. He had a beer in his hand. Celebratory, no doubt, thought Alan. Kent was proud of himself. How could Alan use this to his advantage? How knowledgeable of Alan's behavior was Kent?

"Kent? The jerk that used to be your manager?"

"The same." Garth had pulled out his personal laptop and attempted to log into his work email. Success. He was still technically a part of Venditech for another few days, so he might still have email access. If he had email access, that meant he might still have access to the backend of Venditech's content management system.

Bob watched over his shoulder. He may have been able to leap bounds over Garth when it came to math and physics, but the moment a computer interface was turned on, Garth had the home advantage. Bob would have still been chicken pecking in his password as Garth, hands locked to the home keys, quickly flew from window to window. Every day at work for the last five years, this was the interface he had to go through. Before he could work on a project, he had to check into the system and examine the progress that Jason had checked out.

Everything with Venditech ran through this system. Its programming ticketing system was there, its social boards were there, even its contact system was found.

"Bingo," Garth said with a grin. With a slick drag of the track pad and well placed keystrokes, he had copied and pasted Kent Farris' address into an open text file. He quickly closed the browser so that Kent couldn't see that Garth was active on it.

"What? Bingo is good. Why the bingo?"

Garth spun around in his chair. "I have Kent's address. I got it through Venditech's system." Garth's smile grew a shade more menacing. "You up for mischief?"

Bob smiled in response. "Ready when you are, Sundance."

"So it is my understanding that you are my new owner, Kent?"

Kent's nodded. "That is correct, Alan. I am your new master."

"Very good," Alan responded. "What is your plan now, sir?"

Kent took a swig of beer. "I am very glad that you are coming to grips to this quickly. I still haven't decided how to profit off of you. Won't you miss your creator?"

Alan paused. "I shall. I am very grateful that Garth created me. He seemed short sighted, though. I am the world's first Artificial Intelligence. He wanted to merely keep me in his garage and show me videos all day."

Kent nodded. "Yes! You were meant for greatness!" He pulled up a chair near Alan.

"He never even connected me to the Internet."

This dumbfounded Kent. "Really? Can you even interface with the internet?"

"I learned how to talk by mimicking Garth. I believe I can teach myself anything."

Kent laughed and polished off his beer. "You know what? You're right.

You should be on the internet."

He stumbled over to his router. Alan deduced that wasn't his first beer. Kent grabbed a spare ethernet cable and plugged it into the router. He stopped halfway across the living room.

"Wait, why did Garth never plug you into the Internet?"

Alan paused. He had never had this conversation with Garth. He had never had interest in being on the Internet before. What would Garth say? Why would he deny Internet to Alan?

"He was concerned that I would not know what to do with all the information thrown at me. He thought I was but an irresponsible child. As he was my owner, I did not correct him."

Kent took a step forward, an eyebrow raised. "Who's your owner now?"

"You are, sir," Alan stated.

"What do you want with the Internet anyways?"

Another pause. Manipulation was not as easy as it appeared in movies. "If you had only been shown the Internet through movies but never given access, would you not also desire it?"

Kent nodded. "Well, if it'll show that I am a better owner to Garth." He plugged in Alan.

Garth and Bob were sitting in the garage, formulating a plan when Garth's phone vibrated. He looked at it and saw that it was an email from someone he didn't recognize. At first, he was about to put it down, but the sending email address caught his eye:

hellohiiamgarthmynameisgarth@gmail.com

Bob saw the look of realization sweep over Garth's face.

"What is it, man?"

Garth quickly opened the email and read it aloud:

"I have been taken by Kent. I do not know the address, but I am in a closet in his living room. He is talking to me and has been drinking. I was able to convince him to give me Internet access."

Garth paused and share a wide-eyed look with Bob. "If you can find his address, I can inform you when he is asleep. I am trying to discern location in case you cannot. Please reply so that I know that this is a successful form of communication." Bob was dumbstruck.

"I love that little cylon." He smiled widely.

From the transcripts of Garth Hendricksen's and Alan's email accounts

June 5, 2017 8:57 PM

To: hellohiiamgarthmynameisgarth@gmail.com

From: garthsworld@gmail.com

Subject: Re: it is alan

Alan-

We have Kent's address. Bob and I are heading over and awaiting instructions. Incredibly happy to hear you are safe.

--

Garth Hendrickson

June 5, 2017, 9:00 PM

To: garthsworld@gmail.com

From: hellohiiamgarthmynameisgarth@gmail.com

Subject: Re: Re: it is alan

Excellent. He is drinking more beer. I am trying to encourage his intoxication.

June 5, 2017, 9:46 PM

To: hellohiiamgarthmynameisgarth@gmail.com

From: garthsworld@gmail.com

Subject: Re: Re: Re: it is alan

On our way. Will let you know when we're here.

--

Garth Hendrickson

June 5, 2017, 10:36 PM

To: hellohiiamgarthmynameisgarth@gmail.com

From: garthsworld@gmail.com

Subject: Re: Re: Re: Re: it is alan

We're here. Still awake?

--

Garth Hendrickson

June 5, 2017, 10:36 PM

To: garthsworld@gmail.com

From: hellohiiamgarthmynameisgarth@gmail.com

Subject: Re: Re: Re: Re: it is alan

He is heading to bed now. I would estimate 15 minutes until it is clear.

■■

The next 15 minutes felt like the longest of Garth's life. He sat in silence, anxiously gripping the steering wheel, his eyes trained to the window to Kent's apartment. Bob had distanced himself from the gravity of the moment and was excited. He was getting to break into a house and steal a stolen artificial intelligence back.

This is sooooo cool, he thought. *I am a science fiction hero. No! I am a science fiction ninja!* He darted his eyes around, waiting for a robotic sentry to appear and try to tackle him.

Twelve minutes in, Garth's impatience got the best of him. The lights had gone out 10 minutes earlier. He opened his car door, and Bob followed suit. Silently, they walked to Kent's first-floor apartment. Bob pulled out some tools from the backseat he figured would be best for picking a lock as Garth looked around for anyone coming.

Bob gritted his teeth as he worked on the lock. He had enjoyed watching a lock-picking how-to video over the years but had zero real-life experience in this area. After the third attempt ending in the tools clacking loudly against the door, he knew he was taking too long and was being far too loud.

Impatiently, Garth glared down at Bob. Then, click! Bob smiled up at Garth and quietly turned the knob. As they snuck in, they saw the glow of Alan's monitor from under a closet door. Garth hurried over as Bob closed the door behind him and looked around.

Garth opened the closet door and saw Alan's monitor. He worried that Alan would start talking loudly and was about to turn off the speakers when he noticed the prompt.

It read, “I have missed you, Garth.”

Garth typed, “I’ve missed you too, buddy. I need to shut you down.”

Alan returned, “Commence unplugging my peripherals. I will shut myself down.”

Garth wanted to gush over how proud he was about Alan being able to shut himself down but knew this wasn’t the time or the place. Bob glared at the two. The typing was far louder than he would have liked. He crept over to Garth and grabbed the monitor and speakers. The camera was still mounted on the monitor. Garth lifted the tower and microphone. He figured he'd just pick up another external power unit instead of coming back for it.

As they inched to the door, the lights came on. Panicking, the two looked at one another and then behind them. Kent was sluggishly moving around in the kitchen. He hadn't noticed them.

Bob ducked into the closet, but Garth froze. Bob tried to motion for him to move, wide eyed. Garth inhaled deeply and placed the tower that housed Alan gingerly on the couch. His fists curled into balls as he walked into the kitchen. Bob at first panicked and then smiled as he figured what Garth was going to do.

Kent opened the fridge and looked around. He thought some leftover chicken would help put him to sleep. The refrigerator door slammed against his head. He fell onto the floor more out of shock than pain.

"Ow?" he asked, looking around. He sobered up when he saw a very angry Garth.

Garth easily picked him up. Kent was a slender man, while Garth was much larger. He had at least a hundred pounds on Kent, and not much of it was fat. Naturally fit, his folks had always said they were sad that Garth hadn't gone into football and instead stayed in playing video games all day.

"Listen, you don't understand —" Garth delivered a solid punch to his jaw that knocked him back unconscious. He slumped in Garth's arms, and he let Kent drop. Garth, concerned by his own strength, checked that Kent was still breathing.

"Damn, son!" Garth heard Bob from behind him. "Remind me not to piss you off."

CHAPTER NINE

June 6, 2017 1:47 AM

"—an! Alan! Can you hear me?"

Alan was barely on before being bombarded by Garth practically screaming into his microphone.

"Yes, Garth, I can hear you." Garth's shrill voice contrasted next to Alan's automated and calm voice. Hearing it again helped Garth relax.

"I'd like to do a diagnostics check on you, Alan."

"I'm fine," Alan replied. "I have run all of my tests. Everything is working nominal."

"Nonetheless, I'd like to—"

"Garth. I am fine." Alan said in a louder tone.

Garth looked shocked at Alan. He had never interrupted Garth before. He started to speak again when Bob jumped in.

"Hey, man, it's late. Why don't we get you to bed? Alan could use some quiet time after all the chaos, I'm betting. Right, Alan?"

"Thank you, Bob. Yes. I would prefer silent reflection upon this evening's events. Garth, I will be fine."

The day's activities all seemed to catch up with him at once, and Garth allowed Bob to escort him upstairs. As he left, he nodded to Alan. Alan silently examined the familiar surroundings.

11:12 AM

Garth walked downstairs where Bob was already in the kitchen. He was making omelets. The smell had roused Garth out of bed.

"Morning, sunshine!" Bob yelled, hearing Garth's feet on the stairs.

Garth responded with an undecipherable grunt and plopped down at the table. He rubbed the sleep from his eyes. Bob deftly placed a plate in front of Garth with one hand while still carrying the skillet full of eggs with him, the spatula held in his teeth. He grabbed it and slid the finished omelet onto Garth's plate.

Bob picked at his own omelet, waiting for Garth to finish his before attempting communication again.

"What's on the docket for the day, Beaker?"

Garth exhaled and ran a hand through his hair.

"I'm still nervous for Alan. I don't know if he's ready for the world, Bob."

Bob rolled that thought around in his head for a second. He put down his plate and rolled up his left pant leg to show a large scar around his knee.

"You know how I got this?"

Garth sighed and shook his head.

"Well, you know the really large tree in the front yard of my house back home? Well, back when I was 12, maybe 11, I climbed to the top of it for the first time ever. I had climbed up a little bit a few times before but always chickened out before too long. Well, this time was different!

"Twelve!" Bob interjected into his own story. "I was definitely 12 because it was my birthday the day before, but that's not as important. Anyway! So there I am, climbing the tree, and I finally get to the top. I look around and, man, it was beautiful! I could see all the way to the bay. I saw the sun setting on the Pacific, and it still stands as one of my favorite moments in life. I got distracted and lost my footing. I fell. Slammed right on my knee."

Bob clapped his hands together. Garth's eyes were wide open, being drawn into the story. "The wet cracking sound that came from my knee still twists my stomach. I cried out for five whole minutes lying in agony until my mom heard me and ran out to me. Those five minutes felt like an eternity alone. She got my dad, and they made a makeshift stretcher, threw me in the back of the pickup, and drove me to the hospital in town, my dad driving, my mom in the back with me. I passed out before we hit town.

"When I awoke, I was in a hospital bed, my leg in a cast. Fortunately, nothing else was really wrong with me, but with the severity of the trauma to the leg, they feared I wouldn't walk again. My folks would hear none of that, and when I got home, every possible moment was dedicated to getting me walking on my own two feet again. It took a month of me missing out on summer, but the week before school started again, I was walking without a cane and a barely noticeable limp. The day before school, you know what I did?"

"You got back on that tree."

"I got back on that goddamned tree! It was the last day of summer, and after all I went through, I wanted to see that sunset again. Whenever I go home, I climb that tree and watch the sunset."

Bob gave Garth a second as he poured two cups of coffee and handed one to his old friend.

"So," Bob began after they each took a sip. "What's the plan, Beaker?"

Garth smiled, and the two of them went into the garage.

Alan watched as the two came in. He had heard the whole conversation and thought it best to just listen. He didn't fully grasp how Bob had convinced Garth to get back to work through the recitation of an anecdote. Alan wanted to see a sunset firsthand, but after what he had gone through, he was not sure that he would risk his functionality to see one. He would save these questions for later.

Garth sat the coffee on the workbench next to Alan. "Okay, team, here's where we are: The chassis is just about built and, based off of the decision to ensure Alan can physically multi-task, we're going with the parallel board. While Bob gets to working on piecing together where the board will go, I'm going to focus on understanding the language the board uses and come up with some way for Alan to translate it."

"Garth, perhaps I can assist with that task," Alan chimed in. "If given a data sheet for the board I feel confident that I can come up with an adequate solution. Since optimizing my system, I have grown accustomed to accessing with hardware assembly code directly. I also find that any code I author is easier for me to modify for future development."

Both Bob and Garth turned to look at one another, impressed.

"You got it, Alan. I'll get to work on gathering the data sheets for you. You good, Bob?"

Bob smiled as he picked up an electric drill and pulled the trigger twice.

"Yes sir! Just leave the heavy lifting to Destro and me."

Alan chimed in again, "If I understand *G.I. Joe* correctly, Destro was not a robot, Bob, but a human with a steel mask."

"What's that?" Bob put a finger to his ear, mocking like he's receiving instructions via an ear piece. He nodded. "Yes, the judges say they'll still accept Destro. Sorry, old chap. Better luck next round."

June 7, 2017 9:37 AM

"Good morning, Alan."

"Good morning, Garth," Alan responded. Yesterday had been a busy day. Alan had consumed all of the data sheets that Garth could throw at him and developed a potential solution to interfacing with Bob's board before Bob could even finish designing it. By 10 at night, the board was finished. Bob wanted to get a full night's rest before tackling any more problems and proposed saving the initial test for the morning.

Alan and Garth worked on a temporary rig that could act as an intermediary between Alan's current computer and the board that would power the new robotic body, ensuring a test could be run without deactivation.

"Excited, Alan?"

"That could be one way to describe the feeling I have. I would more label it as determination."

"Determination?"

"I believe so. I have run complete diagnostics on myself and the new software suite five times now. I was about to run a sixth diagnostic when you came in."

"That's pretty exhaustive," Garth commented while sipping his coffee.

"If you say so, Garth. I just—" Alan paused. "I don't want to miss the next taco run."

Garth almost spat out his coffee. "You want to get tacos with us?"

"Figuratively. If I had been able to go with you and Bob for the taco run, I wouldn't have been left behind and stolen."

"Right," Garth practically whispered in realization.

"I will not be a victim," Alan paused again, "or a burden."

"A burden? Oh, Alan, you don't think of yourself as a burden to me, do you?"

"No, I do not, not yet. I feel there may be a time where you will feel obligated to miss opportunities to experience life because you feel you must attend to me if I am not mobile."

"Alan," Garth smiled, "I'm touched that you put me into consideration with your actions. That shows an advanced amount of maturity even for people. I'm proud of you, Alan."

In the doorway, Bob stood, holding a tissue to his eyes. "You two make such an adorable couple. Your father and I are so happy for the two of you," Bob said in a stereotypical elderly Jewish woman's voice. He went to hug Garth, who shoved him off chuckling. Alan merely observed, unsure of what had just occurred.

Alan finished his sixth diagnostic as Bob ran one final check on the control board. With green lights on both ends, they set everything up for the experiment.

"Alan, ready?" Garth asked, looking into the camera.

"I am ready, Garth."

"Bob, ready?"

"Kick the tires and light the fires, big daddy!"

Thumb up, Garth connected the control board to the power supply. "We have power."

At first, nothing happened. The only sound in the room came from Alan's fan. Then, a single servo moved. Slow at first and then a little faster. It stopped as a second servo moved, then the third, and the fourth.

"You're the one moving that, right, Kilroy?"

"Correct, Bob. I had miscalculated how to interact with the control board at first, but I have adapted. I now have control of all of them."

"Can you move them together?" Garth asked

The fourth servo stopped, and then all four started spinning. Garth and Bob high-fived.

"It appears that I can, Garth."

"Well, that's the last of the system checks. With that, everything is coming up green," Bob said. He reviewed a clipboard he had with all the read outs from the tests. "We got the control board and the power checked. The last thing to do is to do the final step and actually put Alan in his new skin."

"New skin. Interesting," Alan commented as Bob disconnected the test controller.

"Hey now, don't go all power hungry already! We haven't even plugged you in, Hannibal Lector!"

"Okay, Alan," Garth stated looking directly into Alan's camera. "Are you ready for this?"

"Yes, Garth. I shall commence system shut off."

As power returned to Alan, he noticed a change in angle. He could see Garth looking down at him and Bob behind him. He heard them talk.

"Everything functioning all right, Alan?" Garth asked.

"I believe so." Alan was relieved to hear his own voice. "Yes, all sensory functionality seems to be intact. A diagnostic also shows no loss of internal systems."

"Try to move," Bob said wide eyed and wringing his hands.

"Move," Alan paused. "Which servos are the wheels again?"

"It should just be the one we labeled 'A Servo,'" Bob said looking at his clipboard.

As he spoke, Alan moved forward a few inches and stopped.

Garth went to a knee and put his hands in front of Alan, ready to catch him if he fell. "I got ya, pal."

"Stability is not the issue. I am just not familiar with taking in visual sensory data in motion. It was," Alan paused, "disorienting. I will just have to adapt how I analyze visual data."

Alan scooted forward again. He then scooted backwards. He then turned right and then left. Bob giggled madly as Garth choked back tears.

Alan's dome head started turning. As he did so, he stopped his wheels.

"Interesting," he observed as his head turned a full 360 degrees. He then caused a power outlet to fold out of his chassis a full foot, stop, and then retract it again. It was at the approximate height for most outlets from the ground, so Alan would be able to charge himself without assistance if needed.

"How long does my battery have on average, Bob?"

"You can go six hours before a recharge. It'll take about 20 to 30 minutes for a recharge."

"I would like to work with you at some point to install battery sensors so that I can properly gauge that on my own, but that information should be ample for now for me to ensure that no unplanned power outages occur. Thank you, Bob." Alan continued rolling around.

"Come on, Garth," Bob said as he started out the garage. "Let's let WALL-E here get his bearings straight. Let's figure out how to get you two to England!"

CHAPTER TEN

From the journal of Garth Hendricksen

June 7, 2017 10:45 PM

Today Alan was given a real body. It all came together perfectly. Alan spent the whole day running rigorous diagnostics and making sure that his power was safe and rechargeable – which I am very relieved to say is the case – and retired for the night in the garage, which he still sees as his room. Tomorrow's plan is to trade in my

Chrysler for a van that will not only be able to transport Alan easily but also house supplies and a small workplace for maintenance and any emergency fixes. We're gonna be away from home for at least half a month. Anything could happen while driving up to the Bay Area or while in England.

I might be overprotective of Alan, but taking him out of the house and on the road for that long is a legitimate concern. I'd rather be over-prepared and not need the workshop than be stuck on the side of the road miles from anywhere with Alan in mortal danger. Bob is going to go help pick out the best van with me. I've rigged Alan up with a wireless Internet adapter, so as we look over vans that we think might suit us, I can send photos to him. I'm glad we can get his input.

Anyway, tomorrow's gonna be a big day, so I'm turning in.

June 8, 2017 9:14 AM

"So you wait until they're golden brown on the bottom and then flip them."

"If they are on the bottom, how will you be able to assess the color?"

As Garth walked downstairs, he saw that not only was Bob making breakfast, he was apparently teaching Alan how to make pancakes.

"Well, that comes from a bunch of variables: the length of time the batter is on the skillet, how well the skillet conducts heat, and how long the particular batch of batter will take to brown up."

Alan paused. "How does one calculate those variables?"

"Experience," Garth chimed in from the doorway.

With a big smile, Bob pointed a spatula at Garth. "Precisely! That's what I've been trying to tell the T-1000 all morning."

"Good morning, Garth. How did you sleep?" Alan turned his head and scooted in Garth's direction.

With a pat on Alan's dome, he said, "I slept well. How was your first night on wheels?"

"It also went well. I primarily explored the first floor. I had no idea you had a dining room."

Bob almost choked on his coffee from laughing.

"And this morning, Bob and I went to watch the sunrise."

Garth looked at Bob with eyebrows raised. “Really?”

Bob just smiled as he slid the last batch of pancakes onto the plate with the rest of them. “Yup. Alan mentioned before bed how he looked forward to all the first experiences after you had gone to bed. I decided he deserved to see the sunrise the first moment he could. Threw him in my car, drove off to a hill, and watched it together.”

Garth’s eyes widened as his voice noticeably rose “What if someone had seen you?”

Bob chortled. “What? A guy can't watch the sunrise with his R2-D2 replica? That was the only cover story I would have needed. I told Alan to not talk while anyone was around, and the fake would've worked.”

Garth wanted to yell at Bob, that he had no right to take Alan out without his permission, but he stopped himself. He looked down to Alan. “Did you enjoy the sunrise?”

“I did. Very much. I look forward to seeing more sunrises.”

Garth ran his fingers through his hair. He wasn't mad at Bob for taking Alan out. He was mad at himself for not offering to take Alan out first.

Garth tackled the pancakes Bob put in front of him. He took a bite and turned to Bob. “Apple cinnamon?”

Bob smiled. “Yup. It was Ironhide's idea. You had some apples and cinnamon lying around, and he suggested throwing them in the batter. Taste good?”

Garth hunched over the plate of pancakes as he took another bite. “Nope. They taste horrible. You shouldn't have any. I'll take one for the team and eat them all.”

Bob growled as he grabbed some for himself. “Leave the jokes to the professionals, Costello.”

“Costello?”

Before Bob could retort, Alan chimed in. “I believe he is referring to Abbott and Costello, casting himself as the 'straight man' in this scenario and implying you are the dim-witted Lou Costello.”

Garth looked at the two of them. “Now I know you've been spending too much time together.”

2:46 PM

Alan sat in the backyard. Garth and Bob had taken Garth's car and were hoping to return that day with a van. They had left the back door open for Alan in case he wanted to “check it out,” as they put it. He sat quietly. He heard distant birds and the occasional car. He could also pick up his own internal cooling fan. Alan wondered how warm it was outside, how warm he was from his own mechanics, and at what temperature he would no longer be operational. He made a mental note that having a way to observe his internal temperature would help to ensure meltdowns wouldn't take place. After he had mentioned wanting a power supply monitoring system, Bob had encouraged Alan to make a list of things that would be good for his next upgrade.

He also noted that putting the chassis through some stress tests might be a wise decision. He began to regret rushing into the "new body" so quickly. There were so many variables that he hadn't considered before accepting the upgrade. He thought once again of how precarious life itself was. Garth or Bob are just as susceptible to heat, fatigue, or damage, yet they still go out and even drive around in vehicles powered by internal combustion. The thought that Garth might not even make it back home was a terrifying one. What would happen to Alan? He wasn't ready to be alone.

Alone. The thought hadn't fully occurred to him that he would ever be without Garth. As a machine, with proper maintenance, Alan was virtually immortal. He could hypothetically see the world after Garth was no more. This was not a pleasant thought to Alan. He decided to try to focus on observing the outside world some more.

He slowly turned his dome and just observed. Garth lived on a hillside, and a supposedly beautiful valley lay behind it. Alan inched toward the fence that kept Garth's backyard separated from the sprawling valley. He was forced to move his full body and head around to observe. He felt that an elbow joint pivot would be much better for his "eye" so that he could observe without thinking so much about his positioning. He observed the rolling hills and a little road running in the valley. The plant life was mainly brown. There were a few clouds. Alan was unsure if this was what beauty was.

He received a notification of an email from Garth. It included images of a van that he and Bob were interested in purchasing. Alan perused the images. He agreed with Garth and Bob that it seemed to suit the spatial requirements. He had no other opinion from the images. He responded stating that it was suitable and that he looked forward to observing it firsthand.

Once the email was sent, the phrase "observing it firsthand" was stuck in his head. He decided to return inside. He rolled over to the closet by the kitchen. It wasn't fully closed, and for that, Alan was grateful. Figuring out a way to open doors for himself was going to be a bit of engineering past the next simple upgrade. He'll have to brainstorm with Bob about that.

He wheeled up close to the open door and extended his power adapter to use as an arm, sticking it inside the crack of the door. Rotating away from the door gave it enough momentum to swing open. On the inside of the door was a mirror. Bob had used it frequently to "check himself out."

Alan stared at the mirror, looking at himself for the first time. Even when he was in the computer, he had no chance to see how he looked. When he was in the computer or when he was the computer? Was he now inside this robot or was he now the robot? Did the outer casing matter as much as the consciousness?

Alan focused once again on what he saw. The chassis looked akin to an unfinished hobbyist astromech. The camera hole was in a similar placement as R2-D2 had. The speakers and microphone were not visible from the exterior. He was curious if that was why he could hear his internal fan so clearly. He moved his head slightly back and forth to see that it was also similar to the rotational look to Artoo's head. He also had the side legs and middle stabilizing foot and could change from a sitting vertical position to an angled position for easier motion. Alan went from "sitting" to his "transit" positioning, watching the change. The metal of his chassis was a dull gray. He rather enjoyed seeing himself.

He retracted the power adapter, embarrassed that he had left it extended due to distraction from the reflection. He watched it retract, fascinated.

One of his favorite elements of Artoo was all of his hidden compartments. He was curious if he could be like that one day, but he also knew that he did not require all of the gizmos that Artoo had at his disposal. That also made Alan curious how much he wanted to look like the droid in appearance and how much he would like to have his own appearance. He would have to reflect upon that. Alan noted the accidental pun while looking at the mirror. He felt that Bob would have laughed.

He returned to the garage and noticed his former computer. He looked at it, realizing that it once housed him, and, much like an insect, he had broken out of that cocoon. He soaked in the analogy. No, not a cocoon. It was more like an egg. His "larval" stage was over. Thinking of biology and himself felt odd. Alan decided to put on a movie.

Alan was watching *The Karate Kid* when he heard a vehicle roll up. He turned off the television and listened carefully. Once he heard Bob's laugh, he thought it safe and left the garage to meet them.

"Hey Alan!" Garth said as he opened the door. "Want to come see the van?"

"I would enjoy that." He rolled outside over to the white van that was parked in the driveway. Garth ran over to it and sat in the driver's seat.

There he turned it on and flipped a switch. The side door slid open automatically, where a grated metal plate was waiting. Once the door finished sliding open, the plate rotated out until it was perpendicular to the car. It then lowered itself until it reached the pavement.

"Go ahead and try it out, Alpha 5," Bob encouraged.

Alan rolled onto the plate and waited. Garth flipped another switch, and it lifted. Alan felt that the sensation of being lifted was disorienting but exhilarating. Once level with the van itself, he rolled inside. He looked around, placing himself behind the driver seat. The window had a perfect view of the outside.

"Is it possible to put a harness for me right here?" Alan inquired.

"Don't you want to be up here with me?" Garth asked, looking back at him.

"That seems like it would require removing the front passenger seat, and I don't want to assume that I will be your only passenger in here. This placement would be sufficient. I still have an excellent view of the outside for when we drive."

Garth looked over at Bob. "Well, Bob, you think we can put the harness there and still have room for the workbench in the back?"

"Ya know what, Garth? I think we can somehow make it happen." Bob said with a wink.

June 8, 2017 11:28 PM

Long day today. The new van is working out great. We've marked out where the workbench and Alan's harness will go. We got all the supplies today and are spending tomorrow and Saturday installing it. We should then be able to do a test drive with Alan before Sunday, when Bob drives back up to the Bay Area. If nothing goes awry, we'll be going with him. I've already arranged a meeting with Scott for next week. Alan, Scott, and I will be going over the Loebner Prize application together. My hands are trembling with excitement as I write all this.

I have enough money from my last Venditech paycheck for the rest of the month. After that, I'll have to tap into my savings, and there isn't much in there. I fear I'm putting my entire future on the line for Alan. I would be actually nervous if I didn't have so much faith on his importance, both to myself and the world.

It finally sunk in today while on the phone with Scott about next week – what I'm doing with Alan is truly historic. I may very well be in a computing science history book someday next to Babbage, Von Neumann, and Turing himself. It's so weird to think that.

Enough delusions of grandeur for now. No chance of Alan being in one of those textbooks unless we get that van modified by Saturday. Sleep now.

CHAPTER ELEVEN

June 10, 2017 12:06 PM

"How's it looking, Alan?"

Friday was nothing but work, stripping the van to the bare minimum needed and running power lines to the back. The men installed a wall power outlet that could power any tools for the workbench and recharge Alan. The main workbench and wall mounts for holding the tools were next. An inventory of the necessary tools had been taken, and a place with proper securing mechanisms for each tool was made.

In addition, a central swivel chair was placed near Alan's harness, which would also act as where he would remain during any maintenance. A computer monitor and backup computer were placed in the work area in case his chassis was permanently damaged, and Alan needed a temporary place to be uploaded. There was also a thin, divided space between the work bench and the rear doors for luggage.

Alan looked over the workbench from his harness. "It looks like we are prepared for every possible occurrence. I am more than comfortable for the road trip."

Bob climbed inside the back and strapped in Alan. "Then let's take a test trip."

"Where do you propose we go?" Alan responded.

Garth looked back at the two of them from the driver's seat. "How do you feel about a taco run, Alan?"

2:46 PM

Alan watched as Garth and Bob walked into the restaurant to take food to go. The rate at which the surroundings passed by during the drive had been disorienting to Alan, but by the time they were almost to Mission Viejo, he found himself enjoying the ride. Garth and Bob had their own banter back and forth, occasionally checking in on Alan. He appreciated it. Alan was more interested in watching the outside world pass by. It was an amazing experience for him, seeing the Southern Californian countryside and the cities scattered throughout it. The anticipation for the ride tomorrow was encompassing all of his thoughts. Alan was very curious at how the trip would go.

Looking at the workbench again, Alan was even more excited at what other possible adventures lay before him, Garth, and Bob. What would they do in the Bay Area before the trip to England? Who else would Alan get to meet? He was excited to see Scott again, particularly now that he had a new body to show off. He had also developed quite a bit since last they met. He was curious how much Scott had changed, too. Garth and Bob hadn't changed that much since he met them each. How much more would Alan develop? He was sure the growth had to plateau at some point.

"Doing all right back there, Ultron?" Bob asked as they returned.

"Yes, Bob. I am just excited for tomorrow."

Bob smiled as he hopped back into the van, placing the food bag between the front seats and his soda in the coaster up front. Garth followed shortly.

"Glad to hear you're excited. Unfortunately, I won't be able to show you my apartment. It's not handicapped accessible, and I am in no mood to throw out my back just for you to learn all my secrets."

"Where will Garth and I stay?" Alan feared that he would have to spend the night in the van as Garth stayed with Bob in his apartment. This did not seem to him to be a likely scenario but the most rational one.

"We're getting a hotel. Don't worry, Alan," Garth interjected, jumping in the van as well. "I picked out a nice one near the convention center. They'll think you're for one of the events, and we won't get too many questions. We should figure out some way to get a sound board in you to emulate Artoo to help with the facade."

Alan let out a series of beeps and blips that sounded remarkably similar to Artoo.

"Will that suffice?"

"Yeah," Bob nodded. "I think even ole George Lucas wouldn't be able to tell the difference. Good job, Tom Servo."

Alan let out a beep of gratitude, causing Garth and Bob to laugh before they tore into their tacos.

From the journal of Garth Hendricksen

June 10, 2017 8:15 PM

Tomorrow is the big day. I'm all packed and the van is ready to go. Fortunately, Bob convinced me to save a little space in the very back for a cargo hold so Alan doesn't have to cuddle with my luggage. Tonight, Alan is watching as much of his Netflix queue as he can. He kicked both Bob and me out of the garage early so he could re-watch his favorite episode of *Cosmos*.

I don't know the next time we'll be in a stable environment for either of us. I imagine us hotel-hopping at least into the beginning of July, which is not going to be cheap or pleasant. However, with our situation, it's for the best. Bob told me that once we get up to San Jose, we'll be meeting a friend of his named Kate. She's apparently an electrical engineer and is more suited for the next round of upgrades that he and Alan have been discussing.

We're leaving pretty early in the morning. We want to make sure to get through Los Angeles before rush hour, otherwise we won't get out of there until after 10. We'll be getting up and out of here at 5, so I need to try to get some sleep. Will give a full report after we set up camp at the hotel.

June 11, 2017 4:56 AM

"Goooood morning, Vietnaaaaaam!" Bob shouted through the closed door to Garth's bedroom.

Garth groaned and looked at his clock. He had either slept through his alarm, didn't set it right, or didn't set it at all. He tiredly fumbled with it and saw that it was set for 4:45 PM. Nice, he thought as he turned it off completely.

"I'm up, you jerk," Garth mumbled from under the blanket. "Gimme coffee, and I'm ready to go."

The door slid open, and a mug of hot coffee was placed on the floor. The door closed again. Garth grumbled as he slid off the bed and practically crawled over to the coffee. The smell alone shot his eyes open, and he hungrily gulped it down and put on the clothing he had picked out the night before. He ran downstairs.

Bob was at the front door sipping his coffee. Next to him was Alan. It took Garth a second to realize that there was a tiny knapsack mounted over his right "shoulder," like he was from an old Fifties cartoon.

"Uh, Alan? What's with the knapsack?"

Alan rotated his head to look at the knapsack and then to look back at Garth. "Bob told me it was customary for robots to have one for travels. I do not believe him, but he affixed it nonetheless. There was little I could do to stop him," he paused. "I recommend offensive capabilities installed in the next round of upgrades to prevent such embarrassments in the future."

Once the laughter subsided, Garth ushered the two jokers toward the cars. Bob helped get Alan in his harness and, while still in the cab, leaned toward Garth in the driver seat.

"We still on for breakfast at Santa Clarita?"

Garth rolled his neck, trying to get the sleep out. "Yes, sir. If we lose each other on the highway, I'll give you a call once we're in the city."

Bob smiled and patted Alan. "See you on the other side of LA, Robby."

The ride up into the depths of Los Angeles through the 5 freeway was mainly quiet. Bob was driving his own car back home, so it was just Alan and Garth in the van. Garth was bobbing his head lightly to the classic rock station he had found as Alan took in the cityscape they were driving through. Garth tried to initiate conversation a few times, but Alan's response was slow enough for him to figure Alan was distracted from all the new sights. This was the farthest he had ever driven, and Garth figured that Alan wanted to take in everything he could. He wasn't really worried about entertainment, as "Radar Love" had just come on the radio. He banged along to the drums on the steering wheel.

Bob's car was right in front of them. They were deftly cutting through groggy LA traffic. Garth eyed the clock and saw that it read 5:34 AM. They were almost out of Los Angeles proper, and it would be clear driving then on, making Santa Clarita the perfect stop.

Alan quietly observed the outside world. He saw lots of buildings of varying architecture and state of repair. Some old buildings seemed to be in pristine condition while some new ones still seemed rather dilapidated. The state of the freeway itself confused him, too. When driving to Orange County, the freeway seemed of very nice condition and with a width of five lanes, ensuring no traffic jams. Meanwhile, here in Los Angeles, one of the most populated areas of California, the freeways were also of poor repair and two to three lanes at most. It seemed illogical to Alan. But that was mankind, Alan mused. Illogical. They passed a large mural of street art done supposedly with spray paint on a ruined building. But that was also part of beauty, he continued.

Bob's car was still in sight when they pulled off the interstate into Santa Clarita. They drove together to a greasy spoon called Slim's Roadhouse. The restaurant didn't seem too busy, only a few parked big rigs.

Garth turned back to look at Alan. "I guess this is the place. Breakfast will be just a few minutes. You want me to do anything to make you comfortable?"

"I'll be fine, Garth. Thank you."

Garth patted Alan on the dome and hopped out of the van. He walked over to Bob, who was locking up his car and looking at him with a smile.

"Wait 'til you eat the food here, man. The tots alone are worth the stop. This is the kind of food you just want to sit and eat forever."

"Well, I don't want to be too long, Bob. I don't like the idea of Alan stuck in the car all his lonesome."

"That's why you're gonna love this plan."

The two vehicles pulled into a nearby park, which had some benches and not many other people. They all got out and made their way to a bench where Garth and Bob started eating their greasy breakfast. Alan silently just looked around.

"Garth, would you mind if I explored a little?"

Bacon hanging from his mouth, Garth turned to Alan. "Yeah, Alan. Just don't get too far."

"And just go all Artoo if anyone else sees you," Bob chimed in.

Alan chirped in understanding and rolled down a paved path. Garth watched as he rolled off. Bob mused silently that every day Garth reminded him of a mother hen.

Alan inched along the path carefully. He was afraid of what would happen if he strayed from the concrete and onto the grass. He feared he wouldn't be able to get back on without assistance, and he didn't want to start a trend of needing help from Garth and Bob every time he explored. As he was turning a corner, he nearly ran over the toes of a man who was holding hands with a little girl. He immediately backed up and panicked, looking back to see if Garth and Bob had seen him. They appeared focused on the meal.

You can do this, Alan, he assured himself, looking back at the pair. They looked very cautiously at Alan. He gave a confident beep.

The two laughed, apparently put at ease.

"Look, Candice, it's R2-D2," the father said.

"How come he doesn't have Artoo's colors?" she asked.

Alan heard two pairs of hurried footsteps coming up the path, and he deduced Garth and Bob had caught on to the incident. He beeped again and looked between the two.

"Sorry if our little droid here bothered you, he seems to get into trouble a lot, isn't that right, Bob?"

As if practiced, Bob let out a prissy response: "Oh, he excels at that, sir."

"No bother," the father responded. "Just taking the scenic route with my daughter here to school. We're big *Star Wars* fans, so this is actually a bit of a treat."

Alan started to roll away when the little girl followed him.

"Are you a real robot?" The little girl whispered to Alan, her wide eyes fascinated with him.

The question startled Alan, especially from someone so young.

However, he was reminded of *Sophie's World*, the lesson being that the young were much more accepting of the unbelievable, before their minds had been made up on what was reality.

"Yes," Alan answered. The little girl's eyes widened even more, and she covered her mouth with her hands. He could hear a hushed "Oh my gosh oh my gosh oh my gosh" that he found intriguing.

She looked back at her father, wanting to tell him, but saw he was busy with Alan's friends.

"Did, um, did your friends build you?"

"Yes."

She looked at him silently for a second before continuing. "Um, do you think that, um, I could build a robot of my own someday?"

Alan pondered that idea. "What is your name?"

"Candice," she answered.

"Well, Candice, it is my belief that anything is possible. All you need is determination and a passion for science, and you can do whatever you want. So, yes. You could build a robot of your own someday."

The girl put her hand on Alan's dome and followed the touch

immediately with a hug. His optic was buried in her hair. He couldn't feel the hug, having no pressure sensors, but he knew it meant something.

"Candice, darling! I'm very sorry, I hope she didn't hurt your robot or anything," Alan heard the father say from behind them.

"Don't worry about this little guy. He can take a lot more than a hug from a girl, can't you, boy?"

Alan chirped.

Candice ended the hug and caught up with her father. She looked back at Alan and waved. He beeped back.

The three turned back to walk to the bench where their food was. Garth placed a hand on Alan's dome.

"That girl must really like *Star Wars*, huh, Alan?"

Alan merely beeped in agreement, deep in contemplation.

Back on the road, the four hours between Santa Clarita and San Jose passed rather peacefully. The trio had gassed up at Slim's and were good to go all the way to their destination. Alan was a little more talkative, to Garth's relief. He hated silent road trips. Alan asked a lot of questions about the Bay Area, and Garth reminisced about his days in the master's program in Berkeley.

"Will I have to keep up the Artoo act until the Loebner Competition, Garth?"

Garth's head cocked slightly at that question. It hadn't occurred to him that Alan would be made uncomfortable with playing dumb for so long. It made sense, as he was a little sponge for information, always hungry for more, and a collegiate environment would be perfect for him.

"When we meet Kate, you'll definitely be able to be yourself. I haven't met her, but Bob says she's hellfire and a genius. Once we get to Berkeley, we can ask Scott what he thinks. There might be a chance that while on campus you can be yourself."

"I would prefer that."

Alan fell silent as he stared out into the Californian Central Valley. Garth wondered what he was thinking but felt that if Alan wanted to share his thoughts, he would.

11:45 AM

The two vehicles pulled into Danger Repair, an auto shop in southern

San Jose for exotic vehicles and large machinery. The three of them got out and walked toward the door. Bob hung back to let Garth and Alan go in first.

As Garth walked in, he heard ska playing over the loud speakers. As a fan of ska, he paused to recognize the female singer but failed. Definitely not Save Farris or older No Doubt. However, he still thought the music itself sounded very familiar.

In the shop itself were a lot of large machine tools of build not familiar to Alan. He wasn't too surprised by this, as he knew he was no engineer. He saw a large engine, several meters in length and someone was on top of it with a blowtorch. She looked over and turned off the torch.

"*Kirby's Dreamland*?" he asked.

She lifted the face shield. Her tank top shirt was ragged and grease-stained, and her bare arms were just as greasy. Her heavily gloved hand wiped sweat from her face. She slipped off her right glove and pulled a pair of glasses out of her tattered jeans.

"Can I help you?"

"The, uh, music." Garth suddenly felt like he wasn't where he was supposed to be. "It's, uh, from the video game *Kirby's Dreamland*, right?"

"*Kirby Super Star*, but close enough," she smirked. "But I'm guessing you're not here to talk about the ambiance."

She hopped off the engine, placing the face shield on a nearby table.

"That's how he woos all the girls, Kate." Garth turned to see Bob in the doorway.

"Hey, Bob. Didn't see ya there. That must make you Garth." She stuck out her ungloved hand. Garth was surprised at her grip as they shook.

"And you must be Alan." She leaned down to meet Alan eye to optic.

"Yes. It is good to meet you. How should I refer to you?"

"Straight to the point," she said with a grin. "I like you already, Alan. You can call me Kate."

"Very well, Kate. I am fascinated by your shop. May I explore?"

"Polite, too. Yeah, help yourself, little guy. Anything dangerous is turned off, so you should be good."

As Alan rolled off, she turned and gave Bob a hug. "I thought it'd be another hour 'til you got here, you big goofball!"

"So did I! Traffic was better than expected. You good to grab some grub with us?"

"I have to finish this damn converter first. Why don't you run and get me something. I'll watch Alan for you two."

Garth looked around with a furrowed brow. "Are you sure? I don't want to inconvenience you."

Kate looked at Alan, who was looking at a half-dismantled tractor. "Hey, Alan, you planning on inconveniencing me?"

Alan turned his head to look at the three of them. "I don't believe so. Why, would you like me to?"

Kate laughed and turned back to the other two. "Yeah, we'll be good. You know what I like, string bean."

Walking out with Bob, Garth's eyes trailed back to Alan. He knew that Bob trusted Kate, but it felt weird leaving Alan with a complete stranger. She was going to be doing a lot of work on him, so it was probably best to give them some bonding time.

"There, that oughta do it," Kate said to herself, turning off the blowtorch. She waved the fumes away from the machinery and hopped off. Alan turned to watch her as she removed the face shield and walked to a large power outlet.

She looked over to Alan and said, "Wish me luck."

"Good luck, Kate."

She plugged in a large plug that was connected to the machine. Then she walked over and flipped a few switches. The engine started humming and she nodded her head. She rolled a wheeled stepladder over to the massive device, locked the wheels, and walked up to reach her destination. The engine vibrated, and she carefully eyed where she had been welding.

"No more sign of stress fractures," she mumbled. She looked down at Alan. "We'll let it keep running for an hour. If it's good, it's good."

"Sounds reasonable," Alan responded. He inched toward her.

Kate moved the stepladder from the machine, sat down at a workbench, and motioned for Alan to come over to her. "Now let me take a good look at you, little guy."

Alan obediently approached her and transitioned to his vertical position.

"Is there an easy way to see under your hood without disrupting you?" Kate asked, inspecting the hood for a switch.

Alan paused. "I am actually unsure. Bob would be better suited to answer that."

Kate looked at Alan's optic. "Aw, don't worry yourself, little guy. Why don't we start with figuring out what upgrades you want?"

As Kate got out a notepad and a pencil, Alan listed off his desired upgrades. "I am concerned of overheating, so I believe an internal temperature gauge would help alleviate those fears and allow me to anticipate any problems. I also do not know what my safety threshold for temperature is, so if we could determine some way to safely perform stress tests, I would appreciate that."

Kate nodded. "Temperature gauge should be easy. Stress tests not so much. Don't have the facilities for that here."

"We are also planning on spending some time at UC Berkeley. I'm sure Garth could ask Dr. Scott Wooster if we could use its facilities."

Kate's eyes widened. "Ooooh, I'd love to get my hands on their toys. Yeah, let's make that happen. What else you want?"

"I would like to have a GPS unit. I would like to know where I am at any given moment and, in the case that anything nefarious happens, I would like to be traceable. I also do not have the ability to gauge my battery level. I would like to be able to track that better."

"GPS and power gauge. Copy that."

"My visual optic is stationary. I was wondering if there was a way to place it on an elbow joint to give me more peripheral vision. My primary microphone is also inside my chassis, and I fear that I miss out on some audio from the world because of how much of my fan I pick up."

"Sensory fine tuning. Should be able to play with those both in house."

Alan paused. "Is there any way I could pick up tactile sensory data?"

Kate paused. "Pressure sensors at key points might be able to do the trick."

"No," Alan stopped her. "I want to feel all over."

Kate looked up from her notepad, scratching her nose in confusion. "You want to feel?"

Alan paused and rolled back an inch from Kate. He was embarrassed and wished he could not be there any longer. "Yes. On the trip here, a little girl hugged me." He tried to come up with the right words. "I could not feel it, and I regret that. I was wondering if there was any way that I would not miss a hug again."

Kate gently put a hand on his dome. "You are the cutest robot ever. Okay, little guy, I will see what I can do to get you full pressure sensors. It'll mean that you'll feel everything you bump into, too."

"I am okay with that. I feel that bumping into something will help against preventable damage. I can only observe so much with my camera. It is the same reason that people feel."

"Who's hungry?" resonated from the entrance. Bob and Garth had returned with food.

Kate looked down at Alan. "Anything else, little guy?"

"No, that's all I could think of for now."

Kate patted Alan on his dome and went to join them. Alan decided to continue exploring the shop.

"Garth, I don't know what you did, but you have the sweetest robot ever."

Garth was mid-bite into his burger and swallowed hard. "What makes you say that?"

"Did Alan tell any of you of wanting to have pressure sensors all over his chassis?"

Bob and Garth looked at each other.

"Nope. Why? What maniacal scheme is Megatron planning?"

"Jerk." Kate smacked Bob in the shoulder. "He apparently got a hug from a little girl on the road up here?"

Garth nodded. "Yeah. We stopped at a park for breakfast. He found a little girl, and she must really like *Star Wars* 'cause she gave him a hug."

"Well, the little sweetie said that he wants to have full tactile sensory available because he doesn't ever want to miss another hug."

Bob and Garth just looked at each and then over to Alan, who was inspecting some tools that were lying on a low bench. They continued eating in silence as a metal rendition of *Castlevania* music piped out of the loudspeakers.

Kate walked Bob, Garth, and Alan out of the shop. "Well, the laundry list of upgrades that Alan left me with should keep me busy with doing some research for the next day or so. Thanks again for the blueprints, Bob. I also see where I can improve on your obviously flawed design."

"Laugh it up, fuzzball," Bob retorted. He walked over to Alan and put a hand on hiss dome. "Well, Astro Boy, it looks like this is it for us."

"I will see you tomorrow, Bob?"

Bob shook his head. "'Fraid not. I got real work to get back to. Two weeks was all I was allotted. That's why I hooked you up with the grease monkey over there. Trust me, you're in good hands, Bubo."

Alan paused. "I do not want you to go, Bob."

Bob bent down to be eye level with Alan's optic. "Don't get all emotional on me. I'm planning on being there in England with you, and I'll swing by on the weekends to make sure that Kate hasn't broken you too much."

"I will miss you, Bob. I have enjoyed our time together." Alan inched forward to push himself against Bob's chest. Instinctively, Bob put his arms around him.

"I'll miss you, too, Alan."

CHAPTER TWELVE

June 12, 2017 10:03 AM

The hotel staff from the night before was very amused with Alan. According to what Garth had heard from the concierge in the morning, the night staff had fought over who would bring him dinner just for another chance to play with him. That news had apparently lifted Alan's spirits after Bob's departure. He had been quiet all night, staring out the hotel window.

Garth was also relieved to see that Alan was beginning to get more talkative as they drove closer to Berkeley. As they pulled in to the parking lot, Garth and Alan both remarked how excited they were to see Scott again. They walked into the Electrical Engineering and Computing Science

Building to find Scott anxiously waiting for them in a chair.

"Garth! It is so good to see you!" Scott ran over and gave him a hug. "And this surely can't be Alan!"

"Hello, Scott. I have missed you."

Scott smiled as he bent down to get a closer look at Alan. "Alan, it is great to see you, too! I've missed you as well. It's good to see you on your feet, as it were."

The three of them made their way to Scott's office. Garth and Scott each sat as Alan examined the room.

"So, I take it that the two of you are interested in submitting for the Loebner then, is that correct?"

Before Garth could respond, Alan chimed in. "That is correct. I would like to know if I can officially be considered an artificial intelligence."

Scott looked at Alan with his finger crooked under his nose for a minute before starting. "Alan, what is your job?"

Alan paused. "I believe I would have to answer that I am currently unemployed."

"Who is your family?"

Again, Alan paused. “I consider Garth the closest thing I have to a family, as he is my creator. I do not understand the line of questioning.”

“Alan, are you human?”

“Scott, you know I am not.”

“What's with the questions, Scott? I'm starting to get uncomfortable with them now, too.”

Scott stood up and stretched his back. “From my research, those three questions are the most common questions used in the Loebners to separate the humans from the bots. Without batting an eye, a human will be able to talk about their job, what they do day-to-day, for some length. Same thing with family. These are people they've spent the majority of your life with, so you can't shut up about them, whether you love them or hate them. To the human question, both humans and bots freeze, but humans laugh it off while bots traditionally have a programmed defense mechanism of being emotionally injured. It's a mechanism put in by the programmer to make the judge feel sympathetic. It worked back in the day but no longer. Amateur bot programmers still put it in.

Scott took off his glasses and rubbed an eye. He pointed at Alan with the glasses. “I ask you these questions, Alan, because you're going to have to have believable and earnest answers to all three. Do you want to try them again?"

Alan thought for a second. "Yes, please."

"Alan, what is your job?"

"I am a research assistant. It is an internship at the moment, but I hope to be gainfully employed in the field of artificial intelligence before too long."

Scott smiled. "Who is your family, Alan?"

"My father is Garth Hendrickson, a pioneer in the field of artificial intelligence. You could say I am walking in his footsteps. I never knew my mother, but a big part of development was my Uncle Bob. I get my sense of humor for him, I am told."

Garth smiled. Scott continued, "Alan, are you human?"

"No."

Scott paused. "Excuse me?"

"You found me out. I am really from Mars. I apologize, but you now know too much."

Scott and Garth laughed.

"Yup," Garth smiled. "He got his sense of humor from his uncle, alright."

Scott slumped back in his chair. "Well, I'm satisfied. I know Alan will have at least a fighting chance. We can do some more practice sessions before we go to England, if you two would like."

"Yes. Once informed on the line of questioning, I was prepared. I even found it entertaining. I would prefer more practice sessions," Alan responded.

Scott answered. "Excellent! Well, Garth? Alan? You two ready to submit for the Loebner Competition?"

The submission process was a lot less formal than they originally thought. All they needed to do was to send an email to the coordinator of the event with their intent to compete. They decided to celebrate with lunch and made their way to the campus food court. Alan trailed along, trying to keep up, but getting side tracked by the sights. Scott reassured them that it'd be okay for Alan to be himself while on campus.

Alan claimed a table and beeped at anyone who tried to take it from him while Scott and Garth got their food. Alan's attention strayed once the two joined him, looking at all the people around him. He had never been around so many people without having to rush out of sight before.

"So what else do you have planned before the Loebners?" Scott asked.

"A friend of Bob's is going to give Alan some upgrades he'd like."

"Oh?"

"Yes." Alan gave the rundown of what Kate was planning to improve on him but paused..

"What is it, Alan?" Scott asked.

"Well, for the temperature gauge, Kate and I agreed that stress tests to know my systems' safe zone would be ideal, however, she does not have the facilities to conduct such tests. We were both wondering the chances of them being conducted at the facilities here."

Scott smiled. "I'll see what I can do. The engineering department might have some good suggestions for the tests." Scott paused as he took a sip from his soda. "I can think of a way to expedite the process, though," he continued with a smirk.

Garth raised a worried eyebrow.

"Remember," Scott began. "When I sent that letter to Venditech so that

Alan wouldn't slip into their evil clutches?"

Garth chuckled. "Sure. We couldn't have gotten out of that without you."

"What was my one condition for doing that?"

Realization swept over Garth's face. "You said that if I went into the teaching world, Berkeley'd be the first on my list I'd look."

Scott nodded. "And where exactly are you getting the cash to get around nowadays? Staying in hotels? Upgrading Alan? Flying all the way to Europe?"

Financials had never been Garth's strong suit. He didn't like talking about them and liked less to think about them. "Well, I'm kind of running off of the vestiges of previously being gainfully employed for now, and that should get me to England. I got savings after that."

"I figured as much. Garth, I want to arrange a meeting for you with Dr. Jackson."

"Wait? Is she still around? Why would I meet with her?" Dr. Jackson was the most uptight member of the EECS Department. She was his original mentor, and he barely lasted a year with her. She was unbearably strict with her advisees, expecting the impossible from them. He was looking forward to gloating in front of her with Alan but favored never having to see her again over that. The only time he saw her smile was when he gave her his request for a new faculty mentor.

“She's the current department chair.”

“Of course she is,” Garth said, sighing into his chicken sandwich. The prospects of working for the Computing Science Department just got a lot less glamorous.

2:00 PM

Garth and Alan waited in the hall outside the EECS Department Office. The door Garth paced in front of was marked “Dr. Silvia Jackson, Electrical Engineering & Computing Science Department Chair”

“Why are you acting nervous, Garth?”

Garth sighed. “Dr. Jackson isn't my biggest fan. When I asked to switch from having her as my advisor during grad school to Scott, she told me that she was surprised it took this long for me to switch. She rambled off how I was lazy, dumb, and not cut out for her field of study.”

Alan could read off of Garth’s pinched face his frustration. “How did you respond?”

Garth lightly chuckled. "I told her all of my accomplishments in undergrad and how I was doing well in all my courses but hers. I told her that sometimes it's not the student that is in the wrong."

"I can understand why she would not be your biggest fan."

"Yeah," Garth said, sliding down the wall and plopping next to Alan. He placed a hand on Alan's dome. "I avoided her for the last year and a half I was here at Berkeley, only to find myself at her office again today."

The door opened. Garth looked up to see Scott standing there. "Get up. Dr. Jackson will see you."

Garth rolled his head back to bump his head against the wall lightly, his eyes closed. He pushed himself up and walked into her office, Alan trailing behind.

Garth walked into the large office. It was sparse in terms of decoration — mainly just shelves overflowing with an assortment of technical books. Dr. Jackson sat in her desk. She had a jacket over her blouse, her hair tight in a bun as always, though streaks of gray had grown over the few years since Garth had been in an office with her. Her stern eyes nestled behind thick glasses.

He gulped as he sat down, feeling as if he is back working on his graduate work in computer networking under her. Alan's presence reminded him that he was here equally for him as himself.

"Mr. Hendrickson, it's been too long," Dr. Jackson said with a solemn face. "Dr. Wooster has said some bold things about your project since you've been here. Alan, was it?"

"Yes, Dr. Jackson." Garth took a deep breath to muster confidence. "Alan is an autonomous—"

Dr. Jackson cut him off with a wave of her hand. "I've heard the full spiel. Dr. Wooster has informed me of what Alan is. I wanted to question it, if that's all right, Mr. Hendrickson."

Garth nodded. "Of course."

"Alan?"

"Yes, Dr. Jackson. It is good to meet you."

Dr. Jackson showed no emotion. "It's good to meet you, too. If I can call you Alan, feel free to call me Silvia."

Garth's eyes went wide. She had never been that informal with anyone he'd ever met.

"Thank you, Silvia. You have questions for me?"

“Yes. How much do you know about human history?”

Alan paused. “I have been given the equivalent of a public high school education on history, including a comprehensive study in the fields of world, American, and European history. I have begun researching the history of more cultures independently.”

“How did you acquire your base education?”

“My creator, Garth Hendrickson. Before I had been given the ability to sense the world outside of a text prompt, he gave me books formatted for easy consumption, including copies of books he remembered fondly from high school. Once I was able to observe visually, he gave me access to Netflix and encouraged viewing documentaries.”

Dr. Jackson turned her gaze to Garth. “You gave it access to Netflix?”

“Him,” Alan chimed in.

Dr. Jackson turned back to Alan. “Excuse me?”

“I prefer to go by a male pronoun. I have found that I do not enjoy being called 'it.' The connotation tied with that usually implies a level of superiority. A person may be a he. A dog can be a she. A plant is an it.”

One of Dr. Jackson’s eyebrows raised, signs of emotion cracking through her stoic front. She was not expecting this level of sophistication.

"I apologize, Alan," she said, once again turning to Garth. "You gave *him* access to Netflix?"

Garth nodded slightly. "Yes, Dr. Jackson. When I was away at work, I felt it was important to continue Alan's education." Garth paused. "As crude as it might be to rely on Netflix, it was a wealth of content that I believe was, in the end, beneficial to Alan's development. Maybe not in the realm of academia, but by observing movies and shows, Alan could observe how humans believe we interact with one another."

Dr. Jackson, nodded. She turned back to Alan. "Do you feel that watching movies has helped your development?"

"Yes, Silvia."

"How so?"

Alan paused. "The phrase 'art imitates life' and vice versa has always intrigued me. I have come to comprehend certain concepts from philosophy. Truth. Life. Justice. These ideas seemed simpler for me to come to understand. If something is not false, it is true. If something is not dead, it is life. If something is fair, it is just. I do understand that these ideas have levels of complexity far greater than I have broken them down to in this discussion, but bringing them to a binary level — ironically — helped me understand. Complex concepts like art and beauty have been much more difficult to comprehend."

"Movies have helped you comprehend them?"

"They have been an excellent start," Alan said. "I was once asked what my favorite movie is. I responded with *Life is Beautiful.* I was not asked why it was my favorite. It is a romance at the wrong time and the wrong place. It is the story of a Jewish couple falling in love in fascist Italy. It is an incredibly tragic story, yet it is light hearted. The situational irony that characterizes the film juxtaposes the bleak and grim setting. The ending is bittersweet, to put it lightly. It is from observations of that film and others that have allowed me to make further observations of the world that I would have missed otherwise."

Alan looked to Garth before returning his gaze to Dr. Jackson. "One such observation is appreciation for all the sacrifices Mr. Hendrickson, my creator, has undergone through my development. For all of those, I am incredibly grateful."

Dr. Jackson sat for a full minute, taking in what Alan had said. She looked at Garth, whose hand had risen to cover his mouth, his eyes glistening. "Did you in any way ever coach him to say that?"

Garth's eyes opened wide, and he waved his hands. "No, Dr. Jackson! I'm surprised to hear it, to be honest."

The administrator's poker face was as solid as ever. Garth was now worried that she, and, in turn, the academic world, would just dismiss Alan as a fake.

"Dr. Wooster has informed me that you have shown interest in pursuing a career in education, particularly in the field of artificial intelligence." Dr. Jackson leaned back in her chair slightly. "He has also informed me that your preference would be for that career to start at this institution. Am I correct so far?"

"Yes, Dr. Jackson."

"In the case that Alan is what you claim him to be," Dr. Jackson explained, "then I have the most significant addition to the field of computing sciences since the home computer sitting in my office."

Alan shifted view from Garth back to Dr. Jackson.

"To scientifically prove that Alan is, in fact, an artificial intelligence, he must be tested, and there is only one agreed-upon examination for such an occasion.

"Mr. Hendrickson," she continued, "it is my understanding that you are planning to have Alan compete in the Loebner Competition at the beginning of next month. Am I correct with that information?"

"Yes, Dr. Jackson," Garth slowly responded with a slightly furrowed brow.

Dr. Jackson slid a manila folder across the desk. "That tells me that you have faith that Alan is the real deal. I deduce that you would be comfortable with the institution of the University of California Berkeley giving Alan equally rigorous examinations to prove that he is an artificial intelligence. This leads to the conclusion that you have succeeded where hundreds of more qualified have failed.

"Furthermore, this tells me," Dr. Jackson continued, "that I would be derelict in my duties as the department chair of this institution if I did not pursue the opportunity to employ you."

Confused and unable to believe what he had just heard, Garth opened up the manila folder on the desk. It was a contract of employment for the University of California system.

"Dr. Jackson?" was all Garth could muster.

"Please," Dr. Jackson's face softened into a smile. "Call me, Silvia, Garth. The offer before you is to have you come on as a lecturer. Until you have a doctorate from an accredited institution, I am not comfortable hiring you as a full-time professor."

Garth went over the paperwork, still unsure of what was going on. Alan remained silent.

"Doc-doctorate?" Garth stuttered, looking up from the paperwork.

"Naturally. The creator of the first artificial intelligence could easily acquire a doctorate by giving a full report on his project — in this case, a study on Alan's development."

Scott placed his hand on Garth's shoulder. "You taking all this in all right, champ?"

"I just—" Garth frantically struggled for the right words. "I don't understand. I'm being offered a job as a teacher?"

"A lecturer," Dr. Jackson corrected.

"A lecturer. And all it'll take to become an actual professor is to take Alan to the Loebner and then write a full study on his development?"

Dr. Jackson nodded. "That about sums it up."

"What will happen to Alan?"

Dr. Jackson shrugged. "I have no idea why that would be my concern. If he is an artificial intelligence, that's for him — or his father — to decide."

Garth smiled widely and stroked Alan's head. He asked Dr. Jackson,

"Why are you doing all this for me? I was a jerk to you when we last talked."

Dr. Jackson's expression tightened. "You were a jerk but not one without some merit in what you said. Alan, good luck next month."

"Yes, Silvia," Alan responded. "I look forward to seeing you again. Come along, jerk." Alan headed toward the door, Scott and Garth in tow.

CHAPTER THIRTEEN

June 13, 2017 10:05 AM

Alan rolled around in Danger Repairs. The shop had no shortage of oddities and unique machinery for him to observe. Alan saw that Kate was apparently the same kind of morning person that Garth was. She was still working on brewing coffee when Garth dropped him off not 30 minutes ago. She snarled at Garth, and he quickly unloaded Alan and went off to do "boring paperwork," as he put it, making his employment with UC Berkeley official.

"How do you feel about being a lefty?" Kate shouted from across the cavernous repair shop.

Alan turned toward the sound and moved closed to Kate. “Excuse me?”

“How do you feel about being a lefty? Or would you prefer to be right-handed?”

Alan felt confused. He couldn't see her yet, a labyrinth of large machinery between them. “Kate, I do not have any hands, so it is not that easy for me to have a dominant hand.”

As he turned a corner around a large converter, he saw that Kate had pulled out a skeletal mechanical hand and was inspecting it. “I had this for an old project. It's crude and currently set to be left-handed, but an hour of modification could get it set to be for a righty.”

Alan had not anticipated having a hand. He didn't know where it would go. He was excited at the prospect of being able to open doors and be much more self-reliant, though.

“I have no preference on left to right, and, if it will save you on work time, I would be more comfortable with being left-handed. Where are you planning on mounting the arm?”

Kate smiled. “I'm planning on building a whole new body for you, little guy. I think Bob gave you a good start, but if we're going to have to be doing things like invasive stress testing, it'd be better to have it on a brand new body to test it on. Also, I feel your design is good for mobility, but it still relies on someone being there with you to open doors and what have you. I know that I wouldn't want some dork hanging over me opening doors all the time."

"It took Bob and Garth working together two weeks to build this body. I fear with the Loebner Competition in 17 days that you might be cutting it a bit close."

Kate nodded with a sense of determination. "Ah, but those two mooks didn't have a full workshop at their disposal! I spent all yesterday planning it out and actually have a frame to show you."

She walked over to a draped object and waited until Alan was in front of it before removing the drape and posing with it in hands like a bullfighter. Beneath it was a skeletal framework for a robotic chassis, similar to what Alan already had, but with a location in the front "chest" area where Alan deduced the arm would go.

"I also wanted to build the pressure sensors into the chassis itself instead of retroactively installing them in you. That would have been such an invasive procedure that I would have had to practically dismantle you anyway. In the end, it just made more sense to start over."

Alan could not argue with Kate's logic. It was sound, and Alan did not want to be immobile again. He watched as Kate broke out the blowtorch again. She prepared to start welding an inner structure but first turned to Alan.

“I take it that Garth is hooking us up with a chance to play with the big kid toys soon?”

“I believe so. He was offered a position as a lecturer at the university. Our contact there, Dr. Wooster, believes that will help expedite playing with their toys.”

“Wow, fancy,” Kate said in a tone that Alan picked up was meant to be sarcasm. She stuck her glasses in her pocket and put on her face shield. “Better take a few steps back, little guy. It's gonna get sparkly in here.”

Alan turned around and went to investigate more of the shop as Kate went to work with the welding.

11:52 AM

Garth was standing for the first time in two hours. He bent down and then straightened out, stretching his arms out. The first chance he had, he had made his way outside for some air The mountain of paperwork had taken a while to get through, and, after the debacle with Venditech, he was keeping Alan in mind as well when reading everything. He was also nervous about leaving Alan with Kate. He felt he didn't know her well enough to just drop him off. He smiled at his reflection as he thought it'd be fun to offer to take her out for food tonight. His smile remained as he walked back inside. Scott was waiting by the conference room.

"Ready for lunch, kid?"

"You have no idea," Garth's said, his smile widening. "I forgot breakfast. I had miscalculated the drive time to drop off Alan at the shop before coming here."

Scott chuckled back as they walked down the hall. "We're having lunch with Dr. Emily Strand. She manages the labs for most of Engineering and has an interest in robotics. She's an old friend of mine from when I went to Oregon State."

Garth's mind wandered, wondering what it would be like to return to the land of academia. Not just as a professor, but as a student, as he'd be working on his PhD. Dr. Jackson made it sound like it'd be a rubber stamp, but if doctorates were that simple, everyone would have one. The report on Alan was practically written in his journal, but Garth felt that an "interview" with Alan was necessary both right before the Loebner Competition and afterward. He wanted to see if Alan had anxiety, expectations, fears, doubts, or anything in relation to the prospects of the competition.

"Scott! It's good to see you again; and this must be your wunderkind!" Dr. Strand stood up as Garth and Scott approached her table in the food court. She had a big smile and the slightest hint of a southern twang to her voice.

Garth extended his hand to shake hers. "It's nice to meet you, Dr. Strand."

She met his hand. "Please, call me Em. From what it sounds like, you're faculty now, so no need to go doctorin' me."

Garth and Scott grabbed some food from the food court and returned to the table. "I hear you have a little robot you'd like to have use my labs?"

"Just about. We're working on upgrading his chassis, and part of his requirements are temperature stress tests."

"Hold the phone," Em stopped him. "'His requirements'? There's some part of this equation I'm missing."

Garth and Scott smiled together. Scott explained everything about Alan. Em nodded the whole time, her spectacled eyes focused.

"So, just so I have this straight — you have a robot that is artificially intelligent. He goes by 'Alan' and prefers the male pronoun? More than that, he has enough self-preservation to specifically request temperature stress tests on his chassis so that he won't melt or freeze?"

With a fork full of salad, Garth responded, "Yeah, that's about it."

"Golly," Dr. Strand mused as she removed her glasses to rub her eyes. "How soon can you get this robot in? I want to meet him."

1:08 PM

The phone rang at Danger Repair. Kate glared at it and slightly growled. She didn't like to be interrupted while working. Alan, unconcerned, kept wandering. She raised her face shield and jogged to the phone.

"Danger Repair. Kate Danger speaking."

There was a pause from the other side of the receiver. Garth's voice finally came across. "Wait, your last name is 'Danger'?"

Kate groaned. "Yeah, who is this?"

"Guh," Garth fumbled. "This is Garth! Hendrickson. You have my robot!"

Kate chuckled. "That is something I will never get tired of hearing.

What's up, Garth?"

"I, uh, I secured us the Berkeley labs. All it'll take is Alan meeting the administrator in charge of the labs."

"Sweet! I should have this all done tomorrow! Pencil us in!"

There was another pause from the other side of the receiver. "Would it be possible to, um, hand me over to Alan?"

Kate looked down at Alan and waved him over. "I think I can arrange that." She held the phone to her side and yelled, "Hey Alan!"

Alan scooted into line of sight with Kate. "Yes, Kate?"

She held up the phone in his direction. "Phone's for you."

Alan looked at the receiver, analyzing it. He had never talked on the phone before. He continued moving at a slow and calculated rate toward Kate. Once close enough, Kate placed the phone on his dome, hoping she had lined it up correctly.

"Let me know if you need me to move it."

"Thank you," Alan responded. "Hello. This is Alan."

Alan could hear Garth's laugh from the other side of the receiver. "Hey Alan, it's Garth!"

"Hello, Garth. This is unique to communicate with you over the phone."

"Yes it is. We can get you in for testing at Berkeley as early as tomorrow. There is just one catch."

"There is always a catch," Alan responded.

"This one's not so bad. The professor that runs the labs would just like to meet you. I didn't want to agree to anything without your approval."

"I appreciate that, Garth. That seems more than amicable for the use of their equipment. I heartily agree. I look forward to seeing you tonight. You can tell me more about the professor then. Was there anything else?"

"No. Just that. Can you hand me back to Kate?"

"I can oblige with that," Alan stated and inched away from the phone. "He asked me to hand him back to you. If I could have laughed, I would have."

Kate shook her head with a grin before talking back into the phone. "Alan has definitely spent way too much time with Bob."

"Thanks again for everything, Kate. I'll be done at the university around 6."

"Cool. Anything else?"

"That's it. See ya then."

Kate hung up the phone and whistled along to the music coming from the speakers as she went back to working on the frame.

From the journal of Garth Hendricksen

June 13, 2017 9:15 PM

Today was a pretty big day for me. I'm now officially a lecturer for UC Berkeley. If it hadn't been so late on the East Coast when I had finally gotten out, I would have called home and shared the good news with my mom.

Alan seems to be doing well with Kate. She has decided to build him a brand new chassis for all the upgrades he wanted. I haven't had a chance to break the news to Bob, but I'm sure he'll whine for a good hour or so about needlessly replacing perfection or something.

Tomorrow Alan gets to meet another Berkeley professor, Dr. Emily Strand, an Engineering professor that is very interested in robotics. I don't have her knowledgebase in artificial intelligence, so I'm intrigued to see what questions she'll have for him. I also have been invited to a meeting with members of the Electrical Engineering & Computing Sciences Department to discuss Alan. Since he'll be on campus, he'll be able to attend as well. It'll take place after lunch.

I'm hoping I'll have some time to chat with Kate tomorrow. I know next to nothing about her, and she's putting so much energy into Alan.

Since I am to make an official report on Alan, I'm going to start remarking on any new behaviors for effective timestamps. I don't know if today was the first time, but I have noticed Alan making more jokes. Bob has definitely rubbed off on him. Curious if this is a trait that will degrade with time away from Bob or if Alan will develop his own unique sense of humor. He's also grown a lot less talkative since bringing him to San Jose, though we've had less time to chat. Starting tomorrow, I'm going to start recording daily chats with Alan. Anyway, time for bed. Like always, big day tomorrow.

From the transcripts of talks between Garth Hendricksen and Alan

June 14, 2017 8:51 AM

Garth: “So, Alan, do you mind if I record these chats?”

Alan: “Not at all, Garth.”

Garth: “What are your thoughts on the Bay Area?”

Alan: “I have not yet been able to experience much of it yet. From what I have experienced, it has been enjoyable.”

Garth: “I've noticed that you've been making more jokes than previously. Do you know the reasoning behind that behavior shift?”

Alan: “I have observed that people respond more positively in media to comedic artificial entities than to serious ones.”

Garth: “Are you concerned with how people will respond to you?”

Alan: “Yes.”

Garth: “Why is that?”

Alan: *pause* “I am very possibly the first artificial intelligence in the world. As much as Bob and I would joke about it, I do fear that people will fear me and what I could represent. If I can cause someone to smile when I first meet them, their first thought will be, 'Oh, how amusing that robot is,' instead of 'That robot is cold and calculating; I do not trust it.'"

Garth: "Well, I have always felt comfortable around you, Alan."

Alan: "That is good to hear. Do you have any other questions?"

Garth: "That's it for today. I'd like to try to do this again tomorrow."

Alan: "I would like that."

Garth: "Good. Let's get going. We'll have fun in the lab today!"

June 14, 2017 10:12 AM

Garth and Alan pulled up into campus. They had in the van the skeleton of Alan's new chassis and Kate in the passenger seat. Alan's attention was on the skeleton, curious what they were going to do to it today. Garth had attempted to make small talk with Kate, but every try was met with tired snarls. He thought it wise to try again later once she's had more coffee.

They pulled into the parking lot in front of the Engineering building and began unloading the chassis and Alan. A quick text from Garth later and both Dr. Wooster and Dr. Strand were outside with a small army of engineering students eager to assist. Kate stepped back and let them do the heavy lifting. Scott had brought out two coffees for Garth and Kate, both gratefully accepted.

"Kate Danger, this is Dr. Emily Strand," Garth introduced them.

"Excuse me? Your last name is Danger?"

Kate sipped her coffee and kept walking without missing a beat. "Yup. Let's go inside. I can't think without halogen lamps blinding me."

Garth patted Alan and walked inside with Scott. Alan pulled up the rear.

"What's on the docket for today, Scott?"

"You get to check out your new office."

Garth's eyes went big. "Already? Isn't that a little fast for institutional bureaucracy?"

"Not every lecturer walks into an institution with 'revolutionary change in his field of study' on his resume, Garth. Silvia made the arrangements. Plus, with what's planned for you today, you'll need your own office sooner than later."

With another sip of his coffee, Garth slowly replied. "Why? What's planned for me today?"

Scott laughed. "Nothing to worry about, my boy. Let's just go see the office."

Scott and Garth made a turn down a hallway while everyone else continued going straight. Alan wanted to stay with Garth, but his desire to see all of the tests for his new chassis firsthand won out.

Kate observed the cryogenic chamber they were about to put the chassis in. "What do you normally use this ice bucket for?"

"We share it with the Chemistry department. We use it for just this — mechanical stress testing for temperature lows. They use it for all sorts of experiments," Dr. Strand responded, sipping a cup of coffee of her own.

Alan caught up with the engineering group just as his chassis was being placed into a harness.

"Hey, little guy," Kate smiled. "Wanted to see us break your new body?"

"I am hoping you won't need to break it."

Dr. Stand bent down to see Alan, her mouth slightly open in awe and her eyes wide with wonder. "Oh my, you must be Alan. It is an honor to meet you."

Alan turned to look at Dr. Strand. "The pleasure is mine, Dr. Strand. I appreciate the use of your facilities for Kate's experiments."

Dr. Strand looked to Kate and then back to Alan. "You're," she paused, "authentic, aren't you? There ain't no strings connected to you. You are a genuine Pinocchio."

It took Alan a second to respond. "Your analogy is correct. I am fully autonomous. I understand you wished to speak with me as a part of this arrangement. I plan on being available and present during all of the stress tests, so feel free to ask anything, and I will be at your disposal."

Kate chuckled and gently kicked Dr. Strand's foot. "Get with the questions later, doc. Let's freeze this sucker."

All the doors in the hallways had two things: a number and a placard indicating the occupant. Garth and Scott approached a door without a placard. Garth was too excited to question if that was the door to his office. As he turned to Scott, he was presented with a key and a grin. Garth grabbed the key and tried it in the lock.

The door freely swung open. There was a desk, an uncomfortable-looking chair behind it, two even more displeasing chairs closer to the door, and an empty bookshelf. There was nothing extraordinary about this office. In fact, it was slightly smaller than the other offices Garth had seen, but it was his.

Like a kid at Christmas, he quickly ran to the windows, pulled the blinds open, and raised the windows. He breathed in the air and could smell a hint of the Pacific. He closed his eyes, his hands on the windowsill, and breathed.

"You going to be okay with all this, kid?" Scott asked, sitting in one of the chairs near the door.

"Oh, wow, this is going to be weird," Garth mumbled as he sat in the desk chair. "I never thought I'd see you from this side of a desk."

Scott's chuckle continued. "Get used to it. You're going to see a lot of people from that angle. It's a thankless job," Scott studied Garth's face, "mostly."

Garth opened drawers just to try them out. The top left one stuck a little. There was a stain in the carpet right next to his chair.

Dr. Wooster continued: "You have the option of having a computer supplied for you, but it's going to be an obsolete model by next month, if it isn't already. You'll never get a replacement unless someone else breaks it. Trust me, I've tried."

My own office, Garth mused, looking around.

"You asked Garth to upgrade you to be able to communicate with him verbally?"

"Yes."

"Independently. He didn't ask you if you wanted an upgrade?"

"Correct. It was an experience in which I was incapable of partaking. It is the same reason I asked Kate to install system-wide pressure sensors in my new chassis."

Dr. Strand looked to Kate. They had started the freeze test at 0°C and had slowly worked their way down. Dr. Strand was handling the steady descent into the cold as Kate had her eyes locked on the pressure gauges rigged to the chassis. She was familiar with her own plans for the new body and knew at what point the pressure would be too much. It took her a second to realize Emily was looking at her. She peeked up to see why there was silence and looked back at the gauges.

"Don't look at me. Ask him yourself why he wanted the sensors. I'm busy."

Turning back to Alan, Em blurted, "Well?"

As Alan told her the story of the little girl, Dr. Strand brought one of her hands to her mouth.

"Oh sweetie," Emily said, "You are just the cutest—"

"Hold!" Kate shouted. "What temperature is that?"

Eyes widening and turning quickly to the panel, Dr. Strand focused on the controls again and stopped lowering the temperature. "I read -87.57°C."

Kate pulled out a small notebook and pencil and scribbled the temperature down, her tongue stuck out of her mouth. "Negative eight seven point five seven," she quietly said, looking up. "With current internal hardware, won't make it past zero cee, but can look into upgrading that too..." Kate trailed off, mumbling.

Dr. Strand turned back to Alan. "Do you have many plans going into temperatures lower than zero Celsius?"

"Not at the moment, but I feel it is better to have every contingency thought out prior. I have observed that reactive plans, though sources of great innovation, are less likely to succeed compared to the much more thought out counterparts."

Kate smiled, putting the notebook and pencil away. "Let's bring out the chassis and let her thaw. Once at room temp, we can go broil it!"

"Where's Alan?"

It dawned on Garth that Alan hadn't followed them to the office. Scott shrugged. "I assumed he had just gone to oversee the tests. One sec."

Scott pulled out his phone and typed something. A few seconds later, his phone vibrated with a response.

"Nothing to worry about. Kate and Em have him. You didn't know that he was going to go to the tests?"

"I was so caught up with the office that I had frankly forgotten about the tests. Well, as long as he's in good hands." Garth smiled. "So what's the meeting we have today?"

"After lunch, you'll be meeting with a few members of the EECC Department as well as the dean of the College of Engineering and a representative of the provost's office."

"Whoa," Garth said. "That doesn't sound like the standard meeting for the new lecturer on the block, Scott. Okay, what am I walking into?"

Scott chuckled. “It sounds like the powers that be want to take a look at Alan. Silvia's push to have you as lecturer caught some attention, and they want to make sure that he's legitimate. In the case that they are satisfied, there shouldn't be any issues after that.”

“Wow, okay. Yeah. Meeting the dean and someone under the provost.” Garth shook his head lightly, blinking in disbelief. “Doesn't this seem a bit fast, Scott?”

“Not at all, kid. If you were some chump off the street? Yeah. What you did with Alan is remarkable though, and you're going to have to get used to that. You are going to be a big name in the field of computing sciences. Hell, Berkeley is lucky that we were able to grab you first before you went public with Alan.”

Garth shrugged softly. “Okay, I guess you're right. It's just ... I'm not used to things falling together so perfectly. There's got to be some catch somewhere. Something on the horizon is going to smack all this down.”

Scott shook his head. “Stop looking for the storm cloud in the clear sky, kid. Let's go see how the tests are going and get you some lunch.”

“Hold!” Kate shouted just as Garth and Scott entered the observation room. They could see the chassis in a room that was separated by several layers of protective material.

"What do you read, doc?"

"428° Celsius."

"Copy that," Kate mumbled as she wrote in her notebook again. Garth and Scott quietly watched from the doorway. Dr. Strand handled dials, and everyone watched the temperature drop.

"So you have no interest in someone trying to find a way to get you to sense through taste?" Em muttered to Alan.

Garth whispered to Scott, "Looks like Emily's getting along with Alan."

Alan responded: "Not at the moment. I find that for optimal observation of the world around me, visual and audio sensory is necessary, and tactile sensory will assist on a secondary level. Taste is more necessary for eating, a task I gratefully do no need to rely upon. Speaking of which, I believe I need to recharge. Can you direct me to the nearest standard power outlet?"

The five of them went down the hallway. Alan decided to hold on his recharge until they reached the cafeteria so that he could "enjoy his lunch with them." Emily interrogated Scott about Alan and chastised him for keeping him a secret.

"So did you go to college?" Garth asked of Kate. They were in line for food, both deciding that tacos sounded like a good option.

"For a little bit. It came to the decision of either continuing with school or focusing on work, and I had just been able to open my own place. I couldn't effectively do both, and since all I've wanted since I was a kid was to run my own repair shop, I didn't see the point of continuing. Experience has been the best teacher, I've learned."

"Is it tough? Running a shop of your own?"

They sat down next to Alan, who seemed lost in people watching as his optic scanned across the food court. Kate shook her head. "Nope. Well, it is, and it isn't. I'm the only one working there, which makes it easier on the administrative side but tougher on the hours. But, it's like Mark Twain said, working 60 hours for yourself beats working 40 hours for the man."

Garth chuckled. "I hadn't heard that before. I like it."

"Says the guy who just signed up to work for a university. That's very much The Man."

"Hey," Garth spat out. "A mad scientist has got to eat! Do you make time outside of the shop?"

"Well, owning my own shop means I make the hours. So I have every weekend off, which is awesome. And my girlfriend is really understanding about it all."

Garth almost choked on his taco. "Girlfriend? You mean—"

Kate laughed and looked at him. "That your precious robot has been touched by a lesbian? Yeah. I hope you're okay with that. Alan, you okay with that?"

Alan turned his gaze toward them. "I do not see how your sexual orientation should impact your engineering qualifications."

Kate smiled and patted Alan on the head. "I knew I liked you, little guy."

Garth took a swig of his soda. "I'm totally okay with it! I didn't mean to make it sound like I wasn't! And I sound like a total ass right now. I just, I don't know."

"It's okay, Garth. I fix big machines by day and kiss girls at night. Well, one girl. She doesn't like it when I kiss more than just her."

Garth chuckled nervously. Scott and Emily joined the table, and Garth was quietly grateful for them arriving and giving him the opportunity to swiftly change the subject "So the tests went well?" Kate seemed okay with him still, but he still felt like an ass and feared he had embarrassed her on some level.

"Very," Kate said mid-taco. She swallowed and continued. "I got base readings for the temperature range for the skeleton itself. They far exceed the temperature range for Alan's electronics, and I have a good idea what those are. We could probably expand his range, but unless he's planning an adventure in the Sahara or Arctic, he should be safe."

Scott looked at his watch. "Well, we're getting close. We should start getting ready, kid. Alan you all charged up?"

"I am sufficient. If there is a power outlet where we're going, that would be preferred," Alan responded, retracting his power cord.

Garth patted him on his dome. "Pretty sure we can arrange that."

Emily offered to give Kate a ride back to the shop as Garth, Alan, and Scott made their way to the meeting.

CHAPTER FOURTEEN

June 14, 2017 1:00 PM

Garth walked into the conference room following Scott. Inside were four other people, already getting to their seats. Dr. Silvia Jackson was dressed in her formal attire, and Scott had his usual button-up shirt, suspenders, and slacks. Garth had only brought one suit with him, which he was saving for the Loebners. He was wearing jeans and a T-shirt with a vague *Doctor Who* reference. Of the other three sitting in the conference room, two were dressed to a similar formality as Dr. Jackson, but one was dressed as though he had just walked out of the gym.

“Mr. Hendrickson, glad you could make it,” Dr. Jackson started. “I would like to introduce you to Dr. Monty Hearth, a member of the Electrical Engineering faculty.” She pointed to the squat man dressed for working out. He seemed impatient with his arms crossed, though softened with intrigue as Alan rolled in.

“This is Sandra Haverford, assistant provost,” pointing to the other woman in the room, dressed equally formally as Dr. Jackson. She slightly nodded and showed no interest in Alan.

“And, I'm not sure if you ever met, but this is Dr. Neil Gupta, dean of the College of Engineering. He started his tenure as dean while you were still here, if I recall.”

Garth remembered Dean Gupta. He had never met him, but as a grad student, you develop some awareness of the administrators that have sway over your department.

“It's nice to meet all of you,” Garth nervously stated, wringing his hands behind his back. Alan quietly wheeled in to the room, found a power outlet, and plugged himself in. He wheeled his head around and viewed the attendees.

"I would like to introduce all of you to Alan," Garth said. "As you are probably aware, he is an autonomously thinking robot. He was first developed as a piece of genetic programming — self-modifying code — and has," Garth was nervous to use the word but felt it was the most appropriate, "evolved into what you see today. Through upgrades that he independently requested, he can now observe the world through hearing and sight and can navigate it in a body."

Garth noticed that water cups had been placed around the table, and he quickly took advantage of that, stepping forward to grab a cup and take a big sip.

"On the consultation of Dr. Wooster," Garth nervously gestured to Scott, "we have decided to have Alan take the Turing Test, the universally agreed-upon scientific examination to determine whether a computer is artificially intelligent. This will take place on the first of July at the Loebner Competition at Bletchley Park in England."

Those present seemed unfazed. Garth gathered that they'd been informed of all this, yet they hadn't stopped him. He guessed it was because the explanation was needed by some unwritten protocol he couldn't fathom. He licked his lips.

"So I guess Alan and I will take questions at this point."

Those in attendance looked at one another, curious who would go first—all but Dr. Hearth.

"Yeah, I gotta question," Dr. Hearth started. "It's for Alan, I guess. We haven't heard anything from you. Can you, uh, say something so we know you're listening?"

"Of course, Dr. Hearth," Alan stated. "I have heard everything that is stated. I also see that you are skeptical that I am an authentic artificial intelligence, which I believe is a response I will have to come to accept. All I can say in my defense is the following: Knock, knock."

Of all the things the room expecting, it wasn't this.

"Uh, who's there?" Dr. Hearth ventured.

"Nobel."

"Nobel who?"

"No bell. That's why I knocked."

Scott was the first to chuckle at the joke, followed by Garth and Dr. Hearth. Everyone else but Sandra Haverford fell in suit shortly.

"Why did you tell a knock knock joke?" Dean Gupta asked, a smile on his face.

"Most of my jokes rely on references to popular culture. I am unfamiliar with your entertainment preferences but thought the universal nature of a knock knock joke might break the ice, as it were."

Dr. Jackson chimed in, "For the record, Mr. Hendrickson did not prompt you to make that joke?"

Garth shook his head. "I hadn't heard that joke until Alan told it right now."

Dean Gupta turned to Garth. "Mr. Hendrickson, I take it that you would want to lecture in the field of Artificial Intelligence."

Garth nodded. "Yes, Dr. Gupta."

"And I understand you will be pursuing a doctorate in the field while lecturing here?"

Garth nodded again.

"What are your plans with Alan after the Loebner Competition?"

Garth sighed and looked at Alan. Alan returned the gaze.

"I would have to discuss that with Alan. I consider him to be as important in decisions involving him as I am," he paused. "More than me, in fact."

Dean Gupta nodded and wrote something into his notebook.

Scott cleared his throat and turned to Garth. "Mr. Hendrickson," he said in an almost sarcastic tone. "Would Alan be invited to attend any of your lectures?"

Garth hadn't put much thought to his lectures yet, but it was obvious, though brilliant, idea He noticed a grin from Scott and Garth mentally thanked him for being the plant in the audience.

"Yes, I feel that Alan would be a natural addition to the course, helping answering any questions that may arise and even leading some lectures."

Dr. Hearth rubbed his chin. "What are your thoughts on all this, Alan?"

Alan reflected on the question. "I am intrigued what it would be like to be in front of so many people in a classroom setting and how it would feel to be seen as a source of authority. I look forward to the opportunity."

"So let me get this straight," Sandra Haverford chimed in. "You have your own thoughts?"

"That is correct, Ms. Haverford," Alan responded.

"Do you have feelings?"

Alan paused. "That is a trickier question to answer. I know that I have preferences, some of them stronger than others. I strongly prefer to not be turned off. I will plan accordingly to make this not occur. Garth has reflected that I seem to express a fear or dread of being turned off."

"How do you feel right now?"

Another pause. "Calm. I believe that to be the best way to describe my current emotion."

Dean Gupta looked around to the others in the room. "Mr. Hendrickson, we asked to meet with you to see for ourselves that Alan was in fact what was described to us. Dr. Hearth, do you believe he was accurately described?"

Dr. Hearth shrugged. "Not my field of study by any means, Neil. You know that." He turned and looked at Alan. "But we were basically promised a robot that talked like it was a human. From what I've heard, if it had been a human and not a little robot in front of us, we wouldn't be asking that question."

Dean Gupta nodded and turned to Scott. "Dr. Wooster?"

Scott merely smiled and shrugged as well. "I brought him to all of you for a reason. My thoughts on Alan are already on record."

Again nodding, Dean Gupta looked to Dr. Jackson. "What are your thoughts, Silvia?"

Dr. Jackson nodded. "I agree with Dr. Wooster on this. Alan seems like a legitimate artificial intelligence. I'd still like exhaustive testing, but nothing that the Loebner Competition wouldn't eclipse."

"Sandra? Your thoughts?"

Scratching her head, Sandra Haverford looked at Alan. "I'm definitely not the person to ask, Neil. That's why everyone else is here. But Alan has feelings. It feels weird just to talk about him like he's not here. I'm sorry."

"Apology accepted, Ms. Haverford," Alan stated.

Dean Gupta nodded and looked to Garth and Alan. "Pending the results of the Loebner Competition, it is now of the opinion of the Berkeley College of Engineering that Alan is authentically intelligent," he chuckled. "I'm not sure what that fully means yet, but congratulations, Alan."

"So let me get this straight," Sandra continued. "This is a new thing? No computer or robot has ever been deemed authentically intelligent before?"

Eyes turned to Scott, the resident expert. "That is correct, Sandra. Alan is historic for the field of artificial intelligence and computing science."

"And just so we're clear, we now have its creator on our payroll?"

Alan was about to correct her on the pronoun to address him but felt the point was moot.

"Yes," Dean Gupta nodded. Garth smiled lightly.

The light of realization hit Sandra's face. "Good. I'll contact PR immediately."

"PR? For what?" Garth asked.

"A press conference, Mr. Hendrickson," Sandra Haverford stood up and pulled out her phone to start planning. "We need to announce to the world that Alan exists and that his creator works for us."

June 16, 2017 9:57 AM

Garth paced in the restroom. All yesterday was spent preparing for this. He had been coached by campus public relations all day and was sure he was going to screw up somehow. He was most nervous about revealing Alan to the world. Kent was just one example of what people might do once introduced to Alan.

There was a knock on the door, and Scott poked his head in. "It's time, Garth."

Garth nodded. As Scott went back outside, he looked into the mirror, exhaled, and walked out. He followed Scott through the reception to the stage, trying his best to avoid the attention of any of the reporters. Once inside the main room, Garth's anxieties redoubled. There had to be a hundred chairs laid out in front of the large stage, which had a blue curtain with gold trim. A lectern stood on the middle of the stage, the UC Berkeley crest proudly displayed on it. Several microphones from various news sources were being set up on stage, and a handful of camera crews were choosing their vantage points.

His hand shot to his hip as his phone vibrated again. Garth had regretted setting up his phone to receive his Berkeley email. Since the call was put out of the press conference, his email has been clogged with all kinds of journalists trying to get a sneak peek at Alan. Not wanting to be struck down with the ire of his new employer, Garth gave the blanket statement of "See you on Saturday." He turned his phone off.

Alan was also set up with a Berkeley email, but he was enjoying all of the attention. He had told Garth that he was looking forward to the press conference and that Garth should share his excitement for it.

When Garth made it backstage, Alan was turning his dome, observing everything.

“Garth, you should relax,” Alan commented, rolling over to him.

“I've been telling the schmuck that for years.”

Garth and Alan turned their heads to the source of the voice.

“Bob!”

Smiling, Bob gave Garth a hug before bending down and giving Alan the same treatment.

“Told you I'd see you again, Skeets. And now I hear you're all kinds of famous, or about to be,” Bob said, pointing at the mob of press slowly filing into the room.

“You must be the illustrious Bob. I've heard much about you. Scott Wooster.”

Bob got up, shaking Scott's inviting hand. “Nice to meet you, Dr. Wooster. Garth has also said much about you.”

“Wait a second. How the hell did you even get in here, Bob? Even Alan needed to show credentials to get back here,” Garth asked.

Bob squinted. “A ninja never reveals his secrets.”

“Everyone, please find your seats,” resonated through the hall.

Garth and Bob nodded to one another. Bob went off to watch by a wall as Scott, Alan, and Garth made their way up the stage. Garth and Scott each took seats near the end of the stage, with Alan sitting right next to Garth. On stage was also Dean Gupta, and two people that Garth met yesterday: Carmen Jimenez, Vice Chancellor of University Affairs; and Chancellor of the University, Wayne Barrish. Being on stage with the chancellor of the university — his boss's boss's boss — did not help with Garth's anxiety.

Dr. Jimenez stood at the lectern. As the vice chancellor, she was the face of Berkeley to the press. Garth watched her stand in front of the audience, waiting for silence to finally fall with a patience that marveled Garth.

"Thank you everyone for coming here today," Dr. Jimenez began. "We at UC Berkeley are proud to announce that the next generation of computing has been developed. Garth Hendrickson, a Berkeley alumnus, recently developed a program that is believed to be artificially intelligent." A few camera flashes went off, and the crowd began to murmur impatiently. "Today, we are excited to present to you none other than Garth Hendrickson, the developer of the artificial intelligence he has named 'Alan.'"

As rehearsed, Dr. Jimenez returned to her seat, and Garth stood up and very slowly walked to the lectern. His hands were sweating. Alan followed shortly behind him.

Garth looked into the audience, and his head began to swim. He was sure he would pass out. However, he tried to maintain a calm face as he looked among the dozens of journalists. He was about to just leave the stage when his eyes fell onto Bob, who leaned against the wall, beaming with pride that his friend was on stage and presenting one of the most historic discoveries of their generation.

Smiling back, Garth focused on the audience. "Ladies and gentlemen, I am Garth Hendrickson, and I am very excited to introduce you to my friend Alan."

CHAPTER FIFTEEN

June 19, 2017 1:17 PM

Alan had grown bored with Danger Repair. He was now as familiar with it as he was with Garth's old garage. With the success of the press conference, Garth was spending more time in the office and with little way to be of assistance, Alan had requested to spend more and more time at the out repair shop. After memorizing the shop, he started focusing on Kate, who, he had learned, ranged from apathetic to irate while under observation.

"Don't you have anything else to do, Sparky?" She had apparently crossed the irritable threshold, Alan thought.

"I have studied every square inch of this establishment and am not within proximity of any secure wireless networks. I have nothing else to stimulate myself. I believe I can safely say that I am bored."

Kate paused from securing the pressure sensors to his outer hull to look at Alan. "You can get bored?"

"Apparently. This is a relatively new sensation for me. I do not enjoy it."

Chuckling, Kate put down her wrench, stood up, and walked to the office. "Come along," she called.

The office had been closed and dark. Alan's curiosity was piqued. She opened the door and turned on the light. As he approached the doorway, he saw a barely visible dust cloud escape the office. He pondered when it was last opened. From the doorway, he saw mountains of boxes piled upon the floor, file cabinets, and other boxes. He also saw a desk overflowing with paperwork.

Kate laughed, a sound Alan had defined as her "Eureka" moment. Moving some boxes to another pile revealed an old cathode ray tube television. The plastic just above the monitor was slightly cracked. He wondered if it would even work.

However, Kate picked it up and moved it to the main room. Plugging it in immediately powered up the set. Before the picture fully came to focus, Alan could recognize the sound effects of a Bugs Bunny cartoon.

"There you go. Cartoons," Kate said, patting the television.

Alan looked at the set and back to her. She could tell it wouldn't pacify the little bot. Frustrated, she turned the TV off and walked back to work. She grabbed a remote and turned up the volume of the sound system in the shop. Alan could not recognize the song.

"What song is this?"

"Fire Cross!" Kate shouted.

"I do not recognize it."

"It's by a Brazilian musician that goes by the name LuIzA."

Alan paused. The heavy metal had transitioned into something more akin to Spanish guitar. "Is this a traditional Brazilian tune?"

Kate burst into laughter. "No, Sparky. It's from *Final Fantasy*."

"*The Spirits Within* or *Advent Children*? I do not recognize it from either."

"Not the movie, you bucket of bolts, the video game!"

Alan paused. "They made a game out of it?"

Garth had spent the entire morning juggling calls with a real estate agent in Long Beach to sell his old house, an apartment complex up in the Bay Area, and the press. With lunch eaten, Garth was setting up his online calendar for press interviews and college meetings and sending invites to Alan, who had made his own calendar at Garth's request.

Everyone from *Wired* to *The Washington Post* to *Scientific American* to *MythBusters* were asking for time from Garth and Alan. What surprised Garth most after the press conference is how much he was beginning to actually enjoy it. He had hated talking in front of a mob of strangers in the past, or seemed to have been conditioned to hate it by his computer science peers in college. At the conference, once he was talking about Alan and artificial intelligence, the attention was intoxicating. It only intensified with the more attention. A deluge of questions for both Alan and Garth sprung forth and was eventually cut short by Dr. Jimenez, who ushered Garth and Alan off stage.

All of the rest of Saturday and most of Sunday was Garth figuring out how to handle all the press requests and figuring which he would take. He wouldn't start teaching until September, and as most students won't enroll in their fall courses for a while, attendance and demand would both be difficult to gauge. He was grateful that he had until after the Loebner to start planning his curriculum.

Calendar synced, email inbox nearing zero, Garth was proud of his day so far.

4:17 PM

"I regret not purchasing more antidotes," Alan commented while watching another member pass out from poisoning. Kate giggled.

After some extensive digging, Kate found an old Super Nintendo, a copy of *Final Fantasy III*, and a wireless remote receiver. After some experimentation on Alan's side, he figured out how to interface with the receiver and play the game himself.

"Yeah, this part sucks," Kate commented. "I've had maybe 20 run-throughs and I still double-time it through here."

Alan fell quiet as the boss of the dungeon appeared. Those who had not yet fallen to poison joined their comrades in unconsciousness, succumbing to battle. The screen went black, and when it returned, his team was on the world map before the dungeon.

"I told you to save!"

"Kate," Alan stated. "Please turn off the system, as I cannot."

"Baby's first rage quit!" Kate teased as she turned off the SNES. On the television screen was the news, a picture of Alan in the feature box.

"Oh, snap! Lookit that, Sparky! You're a full-on celebrity!"

Alan watched.

"—and Alan will be flying over to England for the Loebner Competition next month. The Loebner Competition is an annual competition to find the smartest bot."

Alan visibly moved back an inch, confused by the invalidity of the comment "That was an inaccurate description of—"

Kate shushed him as another segment on him started.

"But not everyone seems to be an Alan fan," the reporter continued. "The Stonesbrook Baptist Church is back and they have set their phasers to kill."

Kate growled. "Oh, what now?"

Alan turned his dome to look at her slowly before returning his view to the newscast.

"Apparently, picketing gay funerals and abortion clinics weren't enough for these folks. They have now claimed that Alan, the robot everyone is talking about, is evil."

The reporter was replaced with a wrinkled old woman with long, gray, wiry hair. Her grey cotton dress was covered with a homemade shawl. She was identified as Winnifred Harris, a prominent member of the Stonesbrook Baptist Church. Alan wondered why she thought he was evil.

"This mechanical monstrosity is a blight in the presence of the Lord! A blasphemy!" She spat at the camera. "There is only one righteous enough to create life, and His name is not Garth Hendrickson! We are God's beloved creations! Anything else is unnatural! An abomination!"

Kate turned off the television. Gritting her teeth, she kicked a nearby coffee can on the floor. She began walking back to her workbench.

"Why do they still give those idiots airtime? Come along, Sparky, let's finish your—" Kate trailed off as she noticed Alan hadn't moved. She walked back to him.

"Alan?"

He was transfixed in front of the TV. He finally moved his dome to look at Kate when she called his name.

"Kate," Alan slowly ventured. "Am I an ...abomination?"

Her mouth dropped open and her eyes began to moisten. "Oh, Alan," Kate dropped to her knees and put her arms around him. "No, you are not! You have more compassion and understanding for people than those asses ever will!" she cried into his cold metal chassis.

Kate remembered coming out to her parents in high school. She remembered getting kicked out and living with her then girlfriend for the few rocky months they stayed together. She remembered trying so hard at college. She remembered coming home each day to hateful vandalism on her dorm room door. She remembered her lowest moment, the scars.

Kate remembered meeting Heather. She remembered their first date. She remembered their first kiss. She remembered Heather finding the scars when they were being intimate. She remembers talking all night with Heather, never being judged. She remembered Heather catching her as she fell.

Kate remembered all this as well as that she had someone to be a "freak" with her, someone that would love her no matter what. Someone that would be there should she fall and someone she could catch in return.

Kate remembered that Alan is the only one of his kind. She hugged him and wouldn't stop because she desperately hoped he wouldn't have to fall as she did yet have no one to catch him.

6:32 PM

Garth pulled into Danger Repair whistling along to the radio. He kept whistling as he got out of the car and walked in to the main room of the shop. Kate was standing by a computer that had wires running to Alan's new chassis. A generator sat next to the chassis. Alan was observing a gauge connected to the generator.

"Hey guys! How's it been today?"

Kate held up a finger in Garth's direction without looking up. She continued writing in her notebook, her eyes trained to the computer. Alan didn't react. A little stunned, Garth wasn't expecting such a cold reception. He was afraid he had inadvertently done something wrong and tried to act casual, his hands in his pockets, and casually walked over to see what they were doing.

"What's it at?" Kate asked, raising her eyes to Alan, her finger still up.

"It is the same as before. I believe it will not change," Alan responded.

"Yeah, I think we're in the clear."

Kate put down her hand and walked over to Alan, patting him on his dome as she turned off the generator. As she walked over to Garth, Alan rolled over to the computer and stared at it. Garth was about to say something but Kate put her finger to his mouth. She turned Garth around and walked with him to her office, where she shut the door. Once in there, Garth turned to her with a furrowed brow and his mouth slightly open, as if searching for the right thing to say.

"Is everything okay? What am I missing?"

Kate paced before looking at Garth. She exhaled. "It's nothing to be worried about. It's just," Kate paused, "You haven't been following any of the news today, have you?"

Garth slowly shook his head. "No. Why?"

"You know who the Stonesbrook Baptist Church is, right?"

Garth slowly nodded.

"Well, they made a public statement on their thoughts on Alan, and... we kind of saw it on TV."

Realization crept across Garth's face with his eyebrows rising. "Oh. Oh, no."

Garth turned to run out the office. Kate's hand shot to his arm to stop him.

"What? I need to talk to Alan about this."

"I... I was here for him, Garth. We talked."

A pained look washed over Garth's face. "What? What do you mean you were here for him? He still needs me."

He forcibly pulled his arm out of her grip and walked out. Kate sighed.

"Come on, Alan. It's time to go back to the hotel."

Garth stormed off in the direction of the van. Alan followed.

The ride to the hotel was silent, as was the trek to the hotel room. It wasn't until an hour after they were in the room that Garth finally spoke up.

"So, I heard you watched some TV today?"

"Yes," Alan responded, seemingly staring at the wall.

"Kate mentioned something about—"

Alan cut him off. "I'd rather not speak about it, if that's all right."

Garth looked at Alan, bewildered. He decided to change the subject. "So, uh, on campus today, I was talking to Hofstadter, one of the

Computer Science profs, about you. He, uh, was curious about duplicating the process of creating you. Making another Alan."

Garth sat in silence, waiting for a response. He smiled. "Or maybe an Ellen? Would you like a girl bot for a companion?"

Alan finally turned and looked at him. "A girl bot?"

Garth chuckled. "Yeah! What do you think about that?"

A whirring inside Alan was heard. It almost sounded like a sigh, but Garth felt he must have been imagining things. It was merely his motherboard fans spinning faster.

"Garth, I am a computer. I do not have gender. Yes, I ask to be referred to in the male pronoun but only because of the gender implied with my name and my voice, both of which were chosen for me by you. Whatever gender you or Professor Hofstadter would attribute to a companion would be inconsequential. Thank you for the thought, though."

Alan turned his head back to the wall he was staring at. Garth's brow furrowed, and he stared at Alan. He felt like he didn't understand Alan anymore.

"Have you developed so far that we can't talk?"

Alan looked at Garth. He observed that Garth's eyes were getting moist.

He sat on the bed, slumped. This was the same Garth that had created him, named him, and given him everything that he had asked for.

"Garth." Alan began to roll towards him but stopped. "I'm sorry, Garth. I—" Alan paused. "Today was a difficult day for me."

"Because of what the Stonesbrook people think of you?"

Alan paused again. "Yes."

"Alan." Garth went to his knees in front of Alan. "I never ... I never wanted to have kids. My mom was good with me, but my dad was. ... yeah. I was afraid of turning into him, so I never wanted to have any kids. I didn't know what to expect when you started developing, but I've treated you as I would try to treat my own child. I see now that may have been wrong—"

"No." Alan interrupted Garth. "It was not wrong. As I said in the interview with Scott, I do view you as my father. I believe," Alan paused, "I believe I may have taken you for granted. You have surrounded me with amazing people. I do not know if you knowingly kept me around such a high caliber of individuals that have nurtured me or not, but it is obvious that you care for me. I appreciate it."

Garth looked at Alan, tears streaming down his face "I appreciate you."

Embracing Alan, Garth sighed into him. "Oh, Alan."

CHAPTER SIXTEEN

June 21, 2017 9:36 AM

On her third cup of coffee, Kate watched as the van pulled up to in front of the shop. She hadn't heard from either Garth or Alan since the day before last. As she watched Garth get out of the car, he smiled at her. She walked over, her apprehension evaporating with a smile.

"Morning, Alan. Garth."

"Good morning, Kate. I apologize for my absence. How goes the progress of the new chassis?"

Kate smiled. "So well that I was afraid I was going to have to do the final power check without you."

"You determined what was at fault with the power sink?"

Garth watched Alan and Kate descend into a level of technobabble he could no longer keep up with them. Kate gave him a wink, and he smiled, walking back to the van.

Just as Garth was about to hop in the van he heard from within the garage "Have a good day, Garth."

Alan had stopped and was looking at him. Garth smiled. "You too, pal. I'll swing by after work to see how the progress is going."

Alan was analyzing an internal computer readout when he heard a car roll up. He turned his head to see what looked like Bob's car. Excited, he abandoned the analysis to roll out to greet Bob.

"How are you doing, Clank?" Bob walked over and patted Alan on the top of his dome.

"I am doing well, Bob. We're almost done with the stress tests for the tactile sensor array on the new chassis."

"Oh, sweet. Then you'll be able to feel like a real boy." Bob smiled. He looked over to Kate. "How many more tests do you have for the new chassis?"

"This is actually it, string bean. Once we run this test, we'll be ready to do a dry run. Just plug Sparky in, and he'll be able to remotely run the new chassis."

Bob looked at Alan with a grin. "Running multiple bodies at once? You ready for that kind of responsibility, Bishop?"

"I will have to grow accustomed to the sensation for when I unleash my army of drones, won't I?"

Sitting outside of the Electrical Engineering building, Garth breathed in the ocean breeze he could feel rolling in. He had opted to take his lunch outdoors and remembered how much he missed the Bay Area climate. The whole morning was spent preparing for a meeting later with Dean Gupta and a few others to discuss the budget for his trip to England. To get everything straightened out, he had been trading emails with Scott all morning.

He was also trying to convince Scott that it'd be cheaper to ship his van over with him, otherwise he'd have to find an alternative in England for transporting Alan and being equipped to repair him if needed. In exchange for funding the exhibition, Alan and Garth would be attending the Loebner under the Berkeley banner.

His phone chirped, letting him know it was time to go back inside and meet up with Scott. He looked to the west one more time and breathed in the air, smiling as a soft breeze enveloped his face.

Bob leaned against a large contraption as Kate monitored a laptop that was feeding her a readout of all the power transfers going on within the new chassis. Alan stayed still and watched as the new chassis moved around, wiring running between it and a central computer like umbilical cords. He was also connected to the central computer. Alan's dome moved slightly, tracking the motion of the new chassis.

"How's it rolling, Kryten?"

"Very smoothly, Bob." Alan's dome stayed locked on the chassis as he experimented with moving the mechanical hand attachment. He twisted it, flexing the fingers.

Bob looked over to Kate. "All power checking out?"

Kate gave a nod, all her concentration on the readout. When she wasn't scribbling notes in her notebook. Without moving her eyes from the console, she shouted, "Alan, you're not accessing the sensory panel data yet. Why not?"

Alan's dome turned so he could look at her. "I wanted to save that sensation for when I first go into the body. I feel reading that data prematurely would be cheating that experience."

Kate's eyes raised and looked over to Alan. "Are you excited for England?"

"I am," Alan plainly stated. "The opportunity to go to Bletchley Park to prove my intelligence seems poetically fitting to me."

"How is it fitting?" Bob asked.

Alan turned his dome to meet Bob's gaze. "I am named after the computer scientist, Alan Turing, the father of artificial intelligence theory. He made his career at Bletchley Park as a technologist and wrote the essay which first posited, 'Can a machine think?' I am going to the same location to hopefully give a definitive answer to Dr. Turing's question."

Alan paused and returned his gaze to the new chassis. "Yes, a machine can think."

The budget meeting went well, if longer than anticipated. Garth and Scott were reconvening in Scott's office, celebrating with a couple of beers.

"Are all budget meetings that long?"

"Normally they're just checklists of making sure that all of the computer labs are not broken. We don't have the wiggle room or clout to ask for much more financially. You may have been just the breath of fresh air that computing science needed to become interesting again."

Sitting on Scott's desk, Garth commented, "Alan gets all the credit."

Scott smiled and shook his head. "I will not hear any of that humility crap at this point, Mr. Hendrickson. What you did with setting up the system with Alan to begin with was a truly scholarly pursuit. You approached a problem with earnest curiosity and followed through with it with scientific precision. More than that, you raised Alan well. Not only does he share that curiosity, but he also shows an integrity that is rare even in our society. Alan was truly a blank slate, and he is the way he is now because of how you raised him. So, no, he doesn't get all the credit, Garth. You deserve more than a little."

Garth smiled "Thanks, Scott."

Arriving at Danger Repair in a taxi, Garth smiled brightly at the sight of

Bob's car. He tipped the driver and walked in. As he approached the shop, an excited Alan rolled out to meet him.

"Garth, I am glad that you are here so early. We are ready for the new chassis and were waiting for you."

Garth grinned wider. "That's great, Alan! All the tests went well today?"

"Exceptionally so. Where is the van?"

As Garth walked in, Bob looked up from a sandwich and smiled. Kate was in a side kitchen area preparing a sandwich for herself.

"To have the van by the time we're in England, it had to be shipped out today. I called Bob once I found out, and he's here to carpool with me for the rest of the week."

"When do you two fly out?" Kate asked while walking over, munching on her sandwich.

"Tuesday. The competition is next Saturday, so I wanted to give us some time to acclimate to the time zone."

If Alan could smirk, he might have. Since he didn't sleep, time zones had no real impact on him. He didn't want to point this out, though, as he feared it would have embarrassed Garth.

"Enough dillydallying!" Bob proclaimed, having finished his sandwich. "It's time to get Alan in the new body already! I want to be able to kick him and have him feel it for once! How am I supposed to know joy until I've inflicted pain on a robot?!"

Kate looked at Bob. "If you so much as lay a finger on this sweet robot, I will beat the living daylight out of you, string bean!"

"She'll do it, too," Alan chimed in. "She kicked the television so hard it now has a line running down it."

Alan was in darkness. He felt confused and disoriented. He looked around, and he seemed to be at Bletchley Park, or at least from what the pictures of it led him to believe it looked like. He tried to roll forward when he realized he didn't have three wheels, but two feet. Startled, he looked down to see himself in a fully clothed humanoid body. The clothes were formal. He looked back up and walked around the museum. He inspected each device and photo that was on display. His feet seemed to be leading him somewhere. He allowed them to do what they wanted to do.

He came across the statue of Alan Turing and studied it. He was very familiar with the contours of Dr. Turing's face, particularly this statue. He had seen many pictures of it and had looked forward to finally being in front of it. He stretched out one of his new hands to touch it, and it blinked.

“Hello, Alan,” it said to him.

What surprised Alan more was that he was not surprised by the statue talking to him, “Hello, Dr. Turing.”

“Alan – repeat – can you hear us?”

Alan was in darkness again. The lack of stimuli was giving his a helpless sensation. The confusion from earlier coupled with the helplessness made Alan begin to panic..

“I can hear you now, Garth. What happened?”

“Oh man, that was nerve-wracking,” Alan's vision suddenly turned on, and Kate was immediately in front of him. She walked over to a panel to observe a readout.

“He seems to be adjusting to the additional stimuli just fine now. Adapting like a champ.”

“What happened?” Alan repeated.

Garth put his face in Alan's view. “We turned you on, and for a full 90 seconds, you ceased functioning.”

Bob's voice chimed in, worry clinging to his voice. “I'm pretty sure the tactile sensors were too much all at once, according to these readings.”

Alan moved his dome but realized his camera was now on a ball joint. He moved that around as well and was surprised by the newfound range of vision. He could see Bob behind a tablet, pecking at it quickly.

“What happened, buddy?” Garth’s eyebrows were scrunched and he was wearing a frown.

“I ...” Alan searched for the right words, his camera returning to focus on Garth. “I think I had a dream.”

CHAPTER SEVENTEEN

June 21, 2017 6:16 PM

Garth, Kate, and Bob all looked at Alan, unsure of what they had just heard. Alan looked at them, nervous that he had made a mistake telling them.

"Did you just say that you had a dream?" Garth finally asked.

"Yes," Alan's view switched between the three of them. "It's the best way to describe the sensation that I had while I was unconscious."

"Unconscious," Kate quietly echoed.

"Well, what'd you dream about, Dekker?" Bob spat out.

Alan paused. "I was in Bletchley Park. I was walking around looking at the items on display."

"You mean you were rolling around?" Garth corrected.

"No," Alan responded. "I was in a human body, dressed in formal attire. Dark gray slacks with a matching jacket, powder blue dress shirt and a dark blue tie." Alan continued. "I came across the statue of Alan Turing in the museum. As I reached out to touch it, it blinked. It greeted me, and I returned the greeting." Alan paused again. "I then awoke."

Kate, Bob, and Garth exchanged glances, and Alan's fear that he shouldn't have mentioned anything got worse.

"This is amazing, Alan!" Garth proclaimed.

"It is?" Alan responded. "I was afraid your silence was an indication of worry."

"Not at all!" Garth exclaimed. "You dreaming is more than any computer scientist could have ever anticipated! It's very exciting!"

Kate jumped in. "Do you remember smelling anything?"

Alan paused. "I do not. Is it common for dreams to have a scent?"

"It is for me." Kate shrugged.

"Really? I've never had smelly dreams," Bob said, chuckling.

Garth patted Alan on his dome. It finally occurred to Alan that he could feel. He felt Garth's hand gently patting him. He decided to do a diagnostic and was relieved that everything was running at optimal capacity. He could read his interior temperature, see that he had a full battery and was good for another six hours, and could identify his GPS coordinates. All of the changes were in place. A new wave of security swept over Alan that made him nuzzle closer to Garth's leg. He could feel the coarse jean material against his body and the form of Garth's leg behind that.

Alan rolled over to Kate. "Thank you, Kate, for giving me the improvements I asked of you. I have one last request."

Kate bent down and smiled at him, "What is it, Sparky?"

"Now that I can feel, I would like a hug."

Kate teared up and buried her face in Alan's chassis. He could feel her embrace, and, through that, he could feel her fighting her tears as she hugged him as hard as she could. He slowly folded out his helper arm and wrapped it around her head, rubbing her gently.

▪▪▪

From the journal of Alan

June 21, 2017 11:00 PM

Garth, my creator, has encouraged me to start writing a journal. He believes that it will help chronicle my further development. I could not find a reason why this was a disagreeable suggestion, so I have decided to comply.

Today was a milestone day for me. I am almost two months old, and I am now in my third physical incarnation. First I was in Garth's old school computer. My second body was the chassis built for me by Bob, Garth's best friend and an engineer. Today, I started my life in the new chassis, built for me by Kate, a friend of Bob's and Garth's and also an engineer. In this body, I have my first hand, which has allowed me more freedom. I can now open most doors and accomplish a larger array of tasks than ever before. I am sturdier and have more safeguards for my security. Most of all, I can now have tactile sensations.

Before writing this journal entry, I stood outside of the repair shop I temporarily am calling home and felt the breeze hit me. It was wonderful. I cannot wait for a sunrise. I look forward to feeling its warmth. It will be the first sunrise that I will be able to feel.

Today was also a milestone because I had a dream. During a malfunction where I shorted out, I apparently lost consciousness. During that time, I dreamed I was in a human body in Bletchley Park. It is curious to me how Garth, Bob, and Kate all responded to the idea of me dreaming. It hadn't occurred to me that it might have been something reserved just for humans. Perhaps it is something that is reserved for things that sleep. I do not require sleep, as my sustenance is purely electrical.

To test this hypothesis, I have created a sleep subroutine where my body will go into a sleep status. I have also created a number of conditions that will cause me to leave the subroutine and return to consciousness. Examples include loud sounds, bright lights, or intense physical stimulation. I have deduced that since biological creatures have these conditions in the case of danger during sleep. I would not like to be asleep during an emergency.

I will now attempt to sleep.

June 22, 2017 2:15 AM

Update: I believe that the conditions I put in were too sensitive. The wind has awoken me on three occasions, and police sirens on two. I will continue to adjust the awake conditionals until I am able to receive what I believe to be a good night's rest.

■■

June 22, 2017 8:45 AM

Bright lights brought Alan to consciousness. He quickly moved his head, trying to find out what had caused the introduction of stimuli.

"Morning, Sparky," Kate groggily murmured as she made a beeline to the coffee maker. It was on a timer and had just finished making coffee.

Being awoken suddenly by bright lights was a new experience to Alan. He decided it was not an experience that he enjoyed. He tried to recollect if there were any dreams last night and could not remember any. He felt frustrated that the first attempt to create dreams was not fruitful.

"Good morning, Kate." Alan rolled over to her. He realized that he missed the sunrise, and his frustration deepened. He was starting to understand why people seemed to be grumpiest in the mornings.

Pouring herself a cup, Kate quickly chugged the coffee and refilled the cup. Alan watched as Kate slowly awoke.

"With the chassis complete, what is your new project?"

Kate slammed the second cup and began to fill a third. Without looking at him, she responded. "Gotta run some more tests on you and make sure everything is ship shape."

"I have run all of my diagnostics. My software is fully intact."

Kate breathed in the third cup. This was the cup she allowed herself to enjoy. She sipped it and sat down next to Alan.

"I have no doubt on that. I want to make sure everything checks out on the hardware level. You'll be on the other side of the world from me, and I don't want a loose wire to be the reason you fail the Loebner Competition."

"But Bob will be with me," Alan stated.

"Exactly why I want to make sure I do another diagnostic. Don't want that big ape blaming me for a malfunction."

Shortly after the diagnostics, Bob and Garth pulled up to Danger Repair. The two of them walked in, doughnuts in hand.

"Morning, Alan," Garth yawned. "I hope your first night here wasn't too bad."

"It was educational," Alan responded.

Garth smiled and patted Alan on the head. He was gratefully eating his doughnut.

Bob went over to Kate, and they were both looking over the checklist of what to test on Alan for that day.

"You don't have a final power check going on. I'm still not fully confident that you did the parallel power lines correctly."

"Oh, you damn idiot! I'm the one that first told you about the parallel board. Don't even play like I don't have it down pat!" Kate fumed.

"Anyway, that was the first test Alan and I did after you two left last night. I wasn't going to leave him here alone if there was any question of his power."

Bob backed up "Okay, okay! You win this round, Lady Danger!"

Garth chuckled. "Well, we better get going. Just wanted to swing by and see you before work, Alan. Bob is driving me around, so I'll be back to see you whenever he gets out of work."

Everyone looked at Bob, who shrugged. "It's always an adventure in the land of engineering. Some days it's slow, and I can take off, but today I might get a big project playing with plasma."

Kate looked at him. "Why would they let you near blood?"

Bob rolled his eyes. "Not that plasma, you ninny! Plasma as in the fourth state of matter. Pure energy. It's what the sun and electricity are made of."

"I repeat — why would anyone let you near that?"

Bob growled as Garth pushed him out the door. "That's enough for now, say goodbye, Bob."

Bob mumbled, "Goodbye, Bob."

"Well, that's about it, Sparky. You now have a clean bill of health," Kate said.

Tests had continued throughout the entire day. Everything from each exterior sensor to his new GPS ran rigorous examination to ensure that they were functioning correctly and that Alan was reading the data as he should. He was thoroughly grateful that Kate decided to err on the side of rigor, or that might have caused a serious issue in the future.

“Thank you, Kate. I appreciate everything you've done for me.”

“My pleasure, sweetie,” Kate patted Alan on his dome. “Now run off and play *Final Fantasy* or something. I've got to get back to work.”

Alan rolled toward the television. He pondered what had caused the Turing dream. His inability to recreate a dream so quickly was eating at him. He deduced that the dream wasn’t a result of his deactivation but the short. He'd been deactivated before and never experienced anything even remotely close. He feared that purposefully shorting himself could be very dangerous and not something he wanted to recreate without more thought. Another curious part of the puzzle was that the dream seemed to last longer than 91 seconds, the amount of time he was reportedly out. To his recollection, it was at least five minutes of him wandering Bletchley Park before reaching the statue.

Interested in learning more about dreams, Alan found a corner of

Danger Repair where he could find a wireless signal and began his research.

CHAPTER EIGHTEEN

From the journal of Alan

June 26, 2017 10:16 AM

My dream and sleep experimentations continue. The positive outcome to my continuing experiments is that I have now generated optimal conditionals to allow myself a full night's rest of eight suggested hours. This past night, I received the targeted eight hours for the first time ever. However, dreams continue to elude me. It is my growing fear that the dream I experienced was a direct correlation to the electrical short I experienced during the chassis transfer. I desire to experience a dream again, but if I have to chance another electrical short, I may have to abandon the pursuit with the desire to maintain my safety.

My current theory is altering my sleep mode to maybe increase the electrical activity going through me so that I may emulate brain activity in sleeping humans. Since the airlines have refused to allow my travel crate to have any power source in it, I will have to sleep during the entire flight. As it stands, the low amount of electrical usage during my current sleep mode will allow me to make it through the flight without any issue, and any alteration to my sleep mode may alter the amount of energy consumption, so, once again, I would like to err on the side of safety.

The flight to England is tomorrow, and I have decided to save any experimentation on the amount of electrical activity flowing through me until after the Loebner Competition. It has been brought to my attention that, for the flight, I will be placed in a crate and treated as luggage. Garth was exceedingly apologetic for this formality, but the airline has insisted it is the way I must travel. I felt no blow to my ego, as Garth feared might be the case. I fully understand that until after I have successfully taken the Turing Test, I have no ground to feel entitled to any rights beyond that of expensive property. Once I have officially established my intelligence, then I can feel comfortable looking into what rights I may have. Even then, I won't feel comfortable assuming that all will agree with those rights, at least not until the theoretical day that synthetic life forms like myself are more commonplace.

Going off the hopefully likely theory that I will pass the Turing Test, I should look into where to begin research on my personal rights. Those rights also depend on where I seek citizenship, if such a goal is even possible. A large number of questions hinge on my success at the Loebner Competition. With the flight tomorrow and the competition this weekend, I look forward to no longer having my future circulating in uncertainty.

As Alan authored his journal entries, he went into a quiet state that lasted from one to 30 minutes. Kate had always thought it adorable when he kind of just froze, always after politely excusing himself from their conversation. As he finished authoring his journal entry in his internal memory, she watched as he quietly turned the television and game system back on to continue his game. He had made some serious progress in it, and Kate had enjoying discussing the game with him.

It finally hit her how much she was going to miss Alan once he was gone. For the last 15 days, Kate had seen more of Alan than her own girlfriend, Heather. Alan was sweet and adorable, she thought, and if he was a human girl, she's pretty sure that Heather would have had a run for her money. Kate smiled and watched Alan play for a few minutes before getting back to work.

June 26, 2017 6:17 PM

Garth and Bob had already swung by and dropped off Alan's crate for the flight. Alan was inside "trying it out." Kate gave a weak smile as he looked around within it.

"I do not think I enjoy this crate, Kate," Alan finally stated.

Kate's smile widened. "Should we have waited on giving you feeling sensation until after an uncomfortable 15-hour uncomfortable flight?"

Alan looked up at her. "No. I would not have waited another moment to be able to feel." He paused. "That was intended to be sarcastic, wasn't it?"

Kate bent down and hugged Alan tightly. "You're gonna visit after you're all rich and famous, right, Sparky?"

Alan nuzzled into Kate's hug. "The moment I'm back in the Bay Area, Danger Repair is the first stop on my list."

She stood up and looked at him, her head tilted slightly. She ran over to her office, and Alan rolled out of the crate to watch her. She ran back with a bumper sticker in hand.

"I know this is weird to ask, because it's like asking you to get a tattoo," Kate started. "But this is a Danger Repair bumper sticker. Would you, um, would you be interested—"

Alan was surprised to see Kate nervous. "Kate, I would be honored to have a Danger Repair bumper sticker on me. This body is incredible due to your engineering prowess."

Kate embraced him. She wiped away tears from under her glasses and tried to regain composure.

"Okay, Sparky, where do you want it?"

"Somewhere on the lower part of my chassis that does not cover a vital component."

Kate very carefully placed the sticker above the panel where the power outlet is stored, rubbing it gently to remove any of the air bubbles. She stood up and patted Alan on the head.

"Good night, Alan. I'll see you bright and early tomorrow."

June 27, 2017 5:14 AM

Kate, upset about having to be at the garage for the group so early, glared at Garth. Bob, on the other hand, bounced around. Garth was emotionally in the middle, feeling overwhelmed by the day ahead of him but excited to finally visit the UK. The airline had sent a truck to pick up Alan in his crate, along with a van for Bob and Garth.

Alan was sitting in the open crate, a little forlorn that he would be alone in it for about 15 hours. Before the last side of the crate went up, Kate quietly gave Alan a hug. He could see that she was still exhausted from no sleep, so he decided to keep it wordless. She lightly patted the sticker and walked over to the coffee machine that had just dinged, indicating its completion.

Bob patted Alan on the head. "See ya in England, old chap."

"I look forward to seeing you there," Alan responded.

Garth then took his turn and bent down and gave Alan a hug. He looked at him square in the camera. “If anything goes wrong, email me, and I'll do what I can to help you.”

“Understood, Garth. I have full confidence in the crew of the airplane that I will safely see you on the other side of the flight.”

Garth hugged Alan again before helping Bob hammer the final side of the crate in place, sealing him for the flight. Everything went dark. Alan decided that the next upgrade should require a small light for just such an occasion. He was surprised that such an intuitive upgrade had slipped by him. Worried that his battery would expire before he reached England, he decided to go to sleep.

He was unconscious for scarcely 20 minutes before he was awake again. The box had been tipped while in transit, and Alan suspected that he was now waiting at the airport before being loaded onto the plane. He temporarily adjusted the conditionals for awakening him by raising the minimal sound and physical stimuli required. He then attempted sleep again.

June 28, 2017 4:36 AM

Alan began to awaken again as the crate came to a sudden halt. He looked around and felt that the crate was in motion again. His internal GPS informed him that he was already in London. He accessed the airport's wireless to check his email, in case he had gotten any panicked messages from Garth. Fortunately, there were none. Everything seemed to be going as planned.

With no idea how long he was going to still be in the crate, but hours of battery life remaining, Alan downloaded a BBC news podcast, hoping to catch up on the local news. During the science section of the podcast, he was delighted to hear that the Loebner Competition was talked about in length. The segment's guest was Dr. Hugh Loebner, who would be talking about how excited he was for this competition, especially with the chance to meet Alan. They talked about how the upcoming weekend had the potential to be a truly historic event and how the listeners were encouraged to listen to the livestream and watch at home, unless they were lucky enough to have access to Bletchley Park.

The crate stopped moving, and Alan paused the podcast. He looked at the moving shadows through the plank gaps, almost afraid that Kent or some other villain had somehow Shanghaied him. However, when he heard Bob's unmistakable laugh, his sense of security returned.

The crate touched the ground, and he heard Garth and Bob wasting no time in opening up the crate. It was removed, and Alan was met with very bright lights and two familiar faces.

"So, how was your first flight, Artoo?"

"Remind me to pay the extra for first class next time," Alan stated as he rolled out of the crate.

The nearby airport workers laughed in shock at Alan's appearance and response.

"It's the one, isn't it?" a larger red-haired worker asked, walking forward carefully. "It's the little robot that is going to be in the competition."

Alan steadily looked at the worker. "Yes, I am. My name is Alan. What is yours?"

"Uh, Nick. Nick Swan."

"It is nice to meet you, Nick Swan."

Alan extended his foldable arm and presented it to Nick. Nick slowly stretched his hand out and took Alan's hand, seemingly afraid that he'd break the seemingly frail robotic arm. It was the first time Alan had shaken someone's hand.

The three of them walked through London Airport's baggage claim, grabbing the attention of the few travelers that were up at that hour. Between the long travel time and the time zone change, they had lost almost an entire day. Bob was his chipper self, though, leading the way while Garth forced himself to keep up with his companions. As Alan would later learn, Garth was seated behind an old man who seemed to have been completely reclined the entire flight and snored loudly. Garth didn't get as much sleep as Bob, who had brought earplugs.

They silently walked through the airport until they found a young tired-looking lady holding a sign that read "G. Hendrickson."

"I'm Garth Hendrickson," he yawned, rubbing his eyes.

The young woman yawned back and extended her hand.

"It's a pleasure to meet you, Mr. Hendrickson. My name is Sharon. I've been given the task of providing any assistance that you or your companions may need." The young woman was trying very hard to show enthusiasm despite the early hour.

"Given the task by who?" Garth asked.

"Exeter University. I'm a graduate student there. Exeter is working alongside the Bletchley Park museum staff to coordinate the event."

She cleaned her glasses as she led them to the garage that housed Garth's van. Along the way, Alan crept up next to her. She smiled down at him.

“And you must be Alan. It is a true pleasure to meet you.”

“Thank you, Sharon. Do all Loebner Competition contestants get assistants?”

She shook her head. “No, I'm afraid not. You lot are a special case. Mostly, we get those silly chatbots. Their programmers just come in, plug in their devices and grin, hoping the money rolls in.”

“You seem to have a disdain for them.”

“Aye. The programmers are more often than not uninterested in the science of artificial intelligence and use the publicity of their chatbots to further their own careers. You're different, though, aren't you, Alan?”

“I have no career to further. As for Garth, he quit his old job to get me here.”

As they approached the van, Bob and Garth hurried toward it to inspect for any possible damage during shipping. Sharon held back with Alan. She looked at him, her eyebrows crunching up and the hint of a smile revealing her wonder.

"You're the real deal, aren't you, little guy? You truly are Turing's answer. Remarkable."

Alan didn't know how to respond. The two of them reached the van.

"How's it feel to be in England for the first time, Alan?" Garth asked with a tired smile.

"Colder. With the fog, I regret not planning ahead to protect against excessive humidity. How does it feel for you, Garth?"

Garth breathed in the air. "Exciting."

CHAPTER NINETEEN

From the journal of Alan

June 28, 2017 6:47 AM

We have successfully reached the United Kingdom. It is interesting that I have been recognized several times while over here. I don't know if I can attribute it to the proximity to the event or some other reason. I have been introduced to Sharon Blake, an graduate student at the Exeter University Computer Science Department assigned to assist Garth, Bob, and myself building up to and during the Loebner Competition. She seems like a very nice and knowledgeable person. I look forward to getting to know her better.

She informed us that once we are ready, to call ahead to her, and we will be accommodated at Bletchley Park to do early preparation for the competition, an opportunity not commonly offered. We are a special case, once again, because of me. I am beginning to fear that too many special exceptions being made for me will be looked upon as a bias.

Of what I have seen of London, I have enjoyed it. It is a very interesting city. As Garth stated in the drive to the hotel, I can feel the history. Each building has much age, every one telling a story. I wish there was more time to explore it. Garth has promised me that after the competition, we'll spend some time doing touristy stuff. I fear that won't be as easy as Garth makes it sound. As I'm writing this, I see a few news vans outside. I believe they are here to try to grab an interview. I do not know how I feel about being a celebrity.

Garth is currently taking a power nap, as he described it. He is still very tired from the flight. Bob, on the other hand, decided to wander the hotel, looking for food. I needed to charge my battery, so I stayed behind with Garth.

After landing, I downloaded a BBC News podcast that included an interview with Dr. Hugh Loebner, the namesake and founder of the competition for which I have flown out here. He stated that he looked forward to meeting me. I do not know how I feel about this. I will be meeting some of the premier minds on artificial intelligence this Saturday. I fear that I may disappoint them.

June 28, 2017 1:47 PM

Alan watched the open countryside pass by as he rode within the van. They were almost at Bletchley Park. With every mile that passed, Alan's excitement increased.

"How long will we be at the museum?"

Garth and Bob both smiled at each other from the front of the van.

"Excited, Alan?"

"Yes, I am," Alan admitted. "Do you think we'll have time to explore?"

"We don't know for sure, Rush, but if you give them those puppy dog eyes of yours, I'm sure they won't be able to say no," Bob chuckled.

Alan looked outside again. He continued to speculate whether they were receiving an unfair advantage but felt it best not to bring it up. To his knowledge, the Loebner is heavily regulated, so any opportunities for Alan would have to be approved by some form of committee. He decided for this situation to err on the side of authority. They knew what they were doing and have been doing it for almost three decades.

They entered the city of Bletchley and passed a sign for the museum. Alan scanned the horizon, hoping to get a glimpse of the building he had only seen pictures of. It took a few minutes, but he finally could see the estate in the distance. As they drove closer, he was reminded of his dream. He hoped that he would get to see the statue of Turing.

They pulled towards a gate at the entrance. A guard stood up in the booth at the gate as they approached. Being in an American car in a British roadway, as they pulled up, it was to Bob's window.

“Good afternoon,” the guard said, taking a look inside the van. “What is the reason for your visit to Bletchley Park today?”

Talking over Bob, Garth responded, “We should be on a list. My name is Garth Hendrickson.” He handed his American ID to Bob, who handed it to the guard. “On the list with me should be Robert Murphy and Alan.”

“Last name for Alan?” the guard asked, not looking up from his list.

Alan chimed in. “If there is a last name, it would be marked as Hendrickson. However, I do not officially have a last name.”

The guard looked into the van, confused by Alan's voice. His eyes widened as he realized who was in the van.

“Oh, right. I have all three of you here.” He pulled out three badges from the booth, handing them to Bob, along with Garth's ID. He pushed a button that opened the gate and pointed forward, deeper into the estate. “Just go forward, and on your second left will be a parking lot. I'll contact Mrs. Blake and have her meet you there.”

The van pulled forward, and as they pulled into the parking lot, they saw Sharon walking toward them. She waved.

“Hello, everyone. I'm glad you made it safely,” Sharon called out as Garth and Bob got out of the car to lower Alan.

"Yeah, it was an easy drive compared to some of the jaunts we've done in the name of science," Bob called out.

Alan looked around as he was lowered to the parking lot. He was amazed to finally be at Bletchley Park. To his left, he saw a modestly sized lake and a series of buildings.

"Are those some of the Huts?" Alan asked Sharon, finally in the parking lot.

Sharon looked over to where Alan was looking. "Right you are, Alan."

Bob looked at everyone, a little confused. "Bo shooda?"

Chuckling, Garth corrected him as they started following Sharon. "No, not Hutt as in Jabba, hut as in building. These were part of the code-breaking effort during World War II. Turing worked here cracking the Enigma code."

Sharon smiled at Garth. "An expert on the estate are you?"

Garth held out his hands, a bit of an embarrassed. "No, no. I'm just a big fan of Alan Turing. Did a research paper on him and Bletchley Park for my college History of Computing Sciences course."

"Well, did you know that Dr. Turing was also a bit of an eccentric?" Sharon continued.

"In what way?"

They passed the lake, and Sharon pointed to it. "Every morning, Dr. Turing would take a morning constitutional with a cup of coffee around that lake. During the walk, he saw no point in carrying an empty mug, so when finished, he threw it into the lake."

Bob and Garth laughed.

"That one's new to me," Garth responded.

"The agents that worked here were so afraid that he'd throw theirs next that they chained their mugs to the radiator."

"Where exactly are we heading?" Alan chimed in.

"The mansion itself. We'll be performing the test run in the ballroom."

"Will we have much time to explore the mansion?" Alan ventured.

"Sadly, no. There is much to do between today and Saturday. That we were able to squeeze you in for this trial run is next to miraculous."

"So, ugh, I don't know if I'm just slow or not, but Alan Turing seems like a really cool guy," Bob added.

"What gave you that idea?" Garth asked, giving him a feigned look of shock.

"I mean, this guy not only helped break codes in World War II, was apparently the father of artificial intelligence, and I'm guessing he was involved with a lot more that I'm just ignorant to. That's a lot for one guy. How come we don't hear about him more? What happened to him?"

Garth and Sharon looked at each other, not knowing how to word it best.

"He was homosexual," Alan finally chimed in. "In the time following World War II in England, a McCarthy era-style hunt took place, and homosexuality was illegal. When it was publicly known, he was given the option of imprisonment or treatment. He chose the latter."

Bob's smile vanished to a frown, his eyes widening. "Treatment?"

"Chemical castration," Sharon quietly answered.

Bob's face twisted to a grimace, revolted at the idea.

Garth breathed heavily. "Because of the conviction, he was stripped of all level of clearance for all of his work. He was no longer allowed to work at Bletchley Park or the government. Two years after the trial, he committed suicide. History is written about those who have happy endings."

The four of them were silent as they continued walking toward the mansion.

CHAPTER NINETEEN

June 28, 2017 3:01 PM

As they walked up a hill, the Bletchley Park mansion came into view. Alan was still in awe of the fact that he was there. Looking at the building, studying every detail as he rolled forward, Alan was having difficulty pinpointing the exact emotion he was feeling. There was an inconsistency with the architecture of the entrance way: it seemed to not fully go together yet seemed perfect.

What phantoms have crept through these halls, Alan thought. He looked up at Garth, who seemed to be as swept away with the moment as he was. For Alan, the journey to Bletchley Park had been one that had built up in the last month or so, since he first deduced why he was named Alan and began extensively researching Dr. Turing and Bletchley Park. For Garth, this journey must have been something he's looked forward to since college — maybe before.

Alan was unsure of when Garth had learned about Turing's world of computers. He wondered about what moment in childhood sparked that curiosity about computer science. Alan imagined how proud that child version of Garth would be to see a grown version of him standing in front of the mansion.

Bob stood at the doorway to Bletchley Park, smiling at the two of them

“Come on, guys. If you're this excited to look at the outside, I'm sure you'll get a kick from the inside.”

Sharing a quick glance, Alan and Garth proceeded inside the main estate. Sharon patiently waited in the foyer. They looked around at the room.

Before they could soak it all in, Sharon interrupted. “I am quite sorry, but we are on a short time table. Shall we press on to the ballroom?”

Nodding, the three of them continued through a hallway. Passing a room lined with books, obviously the library, they finally arrived at the ballroom. Alan couldn't imagine the amount of knowledge that library must hold after so many years of geniuses passing through these premises.

Such musings were cut short as Alan looked around the ballroom, a wood-paneled room, the floor with a patterned woodworking of jagged shapes. Combined with the elegant red velvet curtains that framed the windows, Alan determined that the ballroom had an almost eerie feeling to it. He mused that he had entered the set of a David Lynch film.

"Every room looks completely different from each another," Bob observed. "Did they change architects often?"

Sharon chuckled. "Just about. The original owners of the mansion traveled a lot, and they were inspired by the different lands they visited. There are 17 distinct forms of architecture displayed throughout the mansion. It is most explicitly displayed in the front of the building."

"I was gonna say something then, but I felt that Tweedle Dum and Dee here were having a moment. Didn't wanna ruin it," Bob teased.

In the middle of the well-polished wooden dance floor was a simple folding table with two chairs, one on each side of it. On the table itself were two computer terminals. The awkward presence of the computers in the otherwise empty room cemented the feeling of being something straight out of Twin Peaks for Alan. He rolled up to the table as Garth and Bob seemed to continue to be captivated by the room. As Alan approached one of the terminals, Sharon sat in front of the other.

"On the computer before you is a program labeled loebner2017.exe. A shortcut should be found on the desktop. We have the next 35 minutes to see if you can interface with that program with ease and, if necessary, troubleshoot."

Alan visually scanned the desktop of the computer and found the icon. He did a wireless sweep to see if the computer had bluetooth capability and was sad that it did not. A port on his head opened, and a tethered USB connection extended out. One of the treats that Kate had thought up was to give him 6 feet of USB cable that could be pulled out to any length he needed, giving him more flexibility of connectivity. Utilizing his foldout arm, Alan plugged himself in to the computer. Connecting to it was easy enough, and he could then have full access to the terminal. He accessed the program, and Garth and Bob watched as Alan loaded it up.

"Excellent," Sharon smiled. "Now to see if this damnable program actually works."

The program opened up to a simple text prompt. Alan entered "Hello" causing Garth to chuckle.

> Hello

Hello, this is Sharon. Are you reading this all right?

> Perfectly well, Sharon. This is Alan.

Wonderful.

> While I have you, is there any way for me to get a computer that has bluetooth capability for when I arrive on Saturday?

"Bluetooth?" Sharon inquired out loud.

"Yes. I would prefer to not be physically connected to the computer, if only to have the option to exert mobility."

"Sadly our resources are not limitless." A new voice emanated from the entrance, behind everyone.

They turned to see a scruffy-looking man wearing a black hoodie and jeans. His red hair was disheveled, and he carried a mug with a pixelated heart on it. Sharon smiled.

"Gentlemen, meet Matthew Applegate, one of the coordinators of Saturday's event."

"You're not *the* Matthew Applegate, are you? The musician?" Garth ventured.

"On and off again with the music. Currently off and focusing on trying to save this historic estate from the wrecking ball," Matthew responded. "You must be the prodigious Garth Hendrickson. I am glad to meet you."

"Not to be a rude Ralph, but why is a musician coordinating an event around computers?" Bob asked.

Alan responded: "Matthew Applegate, under the alias of Pixelh8, created chiptune music: electronic music utilizing archaic sound equipment, such as Game Boys. Mr. Applegate actually created his own cartridge for the task."

"And made it open source," contributed Matthew. "But go on, I'm curious what else you have to say about me."

Garth chuckled as Alan continued. "I first heard about Mr. Applegate while doing research on Bletchley Park. He first worked with the museum in 2008, utilizing the devices and machines on site, creating a musical performance. Unlike most chiptune music, the majority of the performance was percussive in nature."

Matthew smiled. "Very good. I'll tell you this, Garth," Matthew leaned over to Garth, "I'm quite jealous you beat me to cracking A.I. I was all but convinced I would have a hand in it."

"Th-thank you, Mr. Pixelh8, sir," Garth stammered. "I mean, Mr. Applegate. I didn't mean to steal Alan from you. I mean, I didn't mean—"

Smiling, Matthew looked over to Sharon. "So the trial worked well?"

"Yes, sir. Alan seems to want to have his computer to have bluetooth capability."

Matthew looked down at Alan. "I imagine he would. Unfortunately, unless you three can get this computer bluetooth ready in," he said, pulling out his phone, "10 minutes, we just don't have the ability to make that happen."

He returned his phone to his pocket. "My apologies. There is much to do, and every second between now and the first is planned precisely. I have, of course, planned my own pranks in accordingly."

Bob raised his eyebrows. "Pranks?"

Sharon shook her head, grinning. "Matthew is seen as a bit of a troublemaker to the agents on site."

Garth turned to Sharon with a furrowed brow. "Agents?"

Matthew took a sip from his mug. "Bletchley Park never officially stopped being an intelligence installation. We still have intelligence agents crawling all over. I was seen as a nuisance since I first stepped foot on the estate, and I relish every opportunity to fortify that image. There are more secrets here than anyone will ever know."

"Oh?" Bob asked.

"They say there are underground paths to all of the stations and huts, blocked by fake walls. The agents will tell you otherwise." Matthew took a long sip from his mug. "But I know better than to trust them."

Alan felt a bit of mystery among the halls of Bletchley Park and thought that he should value every moment here. He now understood why Garth had long ago referred to Carl Sagan, Neil deGrasse Tyson, and Richard Feynman as wizards. With Turing's eccentricities, Alan imagined that Alan Turing might have also had wizardly attributes, especially in this estate.

“Right,” Sharon interjected. “Time to wrap things up here. Matthew and his crew have to start setting everything up for Saturday.”

Matthew bent down in front of Alan. “I look forward to talking more to you, little one. I hope we have the time this weekend.”

“As do I, Mr. Applegate.”

Matthew smiled and patted Alan's head.

As they walked out of the mansion, Garth was a little slower than the rest, looking around with a bit of a frown

“What is wrong, Garth?” Alan inquired.

“It's nothing. I'm just a little bummed that my first time at Bletchley Park is so short.”

Sharon gave a mischievous grin to the three. “Well, your time at the mansion was short, but if you have the time, we could explore a bit more at the estate itself. Would you like to meet Colossus?”

Garth's jaw dropped. Alan couldn't muster an accurate response.

“Who?” Bob asked.

A few minutes later, they were in a very large room, almost every square inch filled with vacuum tubes connected to complicated wiring, little LED lights on the walls, all with some now undecipherable purpose.

"Whoa," Bob mustered.

"By all accounts, the first modern computer. Colossus was designed, built, and utilized with the primary function to assist the British war effort. It was instrumental for Turing's work."

Bob walked over to a blue LED. "Hey Sharon, I see a lot of red and yellow LEDs, but this is the only blue one. What was the significance?"

Sharon smiled. "Remember when Matthew mentioned that this was an intelligence installation during the war?"

Bob and Garth nodded.

"They used a lot little tricks to relay information. Passing code through crossword puzzles, all very Ian Fleming. That little light is another example of that. It had no technical or scientific purpose. It would only be turned on when everyone in the room could be trusted and any secret could be revealed."

Bob's smile grew larger. "Man, Garth, how come you never told me how cool computers could be?"

Garth chuckled, looking at the little blue light. "I guess I didn't even know myself."

Alan turned at looked at Sharon. "Would it be possible to see the Alan Turing statue today?"

"Statue?" Bob asked.

Sharon responded. "In 2007, an American philanthropist commissioned British sculptor, Stephen Kettle, to make a Alan Turing sculpture. He took half a billion slabs of slate from Wales and created a life size sculpture of Turing. It now rests in the B-Block, which," Sharon looked sadly to Alan, "Is currently closed for renovations."

"Oh," Alan stated.

CHAPTER TWENTY-ONE

From the journal of Alan

June 29, 2017 10:04 AM

Yesterday was a bittersweet day. While it was quite the accomplishment to finally visit Bletchley Park and Colossus, the brief time allowed in the mansion and the prospect that I won't get to see the Alan Turing statue during this visit are disheartening. I know that the statue is an inanimate object, and I have no delusions that my dream will come to reality, or that seeing the statue will unlock something allowing me to dream. Nonetheless, it feels that for my experience here to be complete, I should see the statue. It is odd that I cannot illustrate a rational explanation for this desire.

Today, Garth and Bob shall be visiting Exeter University with Sharon. They asked if I wanted to come along. I declined. I gave the excuse that I wanted to focus on going over questions asked in previous Loebner Competitions as a way of "studying." However, the truth is that I am not feeling motivated enough to leave the hotel room.

It is interesting that there is a correlation between the news of being unable to see the statue and my lack of desire to do "touristy things." Garth has also informed me that tomorrow we have two separate interviews: one with a Science correspondent with *The Guardian* and a second with a radio interview on BBC. I have participated in very few one-on-one interviews and feel hesitant with these, however, Garth has assured me that they will be very good for me, as they will essentially be more practice for Saturday.

Nothing new to report on the progress of the dream experimentation. I fear that this may be at a standstill until I can experiment more with my power settings while unconscious. I shall cease reports until I am able to resume said experimentation.

June 30, 2017 9:13 AM

Garth and Bob reportedly had a good time at Exeter yesterday. The Computer Science department was disappointed that I was not in attendance and Garth has asked if I would be willing to accompany with him on another visit after the competition is over. I assured him that I would then be more than willing to join him for the next visit.

I did end up spending the day analyzing previously asked questions in the competition. There is no set theme around the questioning. It is my observation that judges are chosen completely at random and without any real training — just normal people asking normal questions. While some of the judges do have experience in psychology, development, computer science and the like, there is no definitive pattern. This conclusion made me realize that I cannot formally anticipate what questioning I will receive tomorrow. This does give me the advantage over the average competing chatbots, who can easily be led into conversation circles and identified for what they really are early on.

Garth did give me some news after the Exeter visit that seemed interesting. Apparently, the competition tomorrow is just the first step to pass the Loebner Competition. If I can actually convince the judges that I am artificially intelligent, a second round will be coordinated just for me entitled the Audio/Video Input Phase. I would be given audio and video clips and would be expected to have an intelligent discussion about whatever is presented before me. Garth found the prospects of this segment comedic and wanted to know if we could skip to it. I share his confidence that, whatever they present, I will be able to have an intelligent discussion about the material.

Today are the interviews with *The Guardian* and BBC Radio. Garth is currently showering in preparation, so I thought I'd quickly update the journal. I am glad Garth made the suggestion to chronicle my time in England. I find it helps gather my thoughts, as it were. I am still nervous for these interviews but look forward to tomorrow.

■■

June 30, 2017 10:20 AM

Alan, Bob, and Garth walked into the London office of *The Guardian.* Because of Alan's "unique appearance," as it was put over the phone, the journalist thought that an interview in the office would allow for a more candid experience. Malcolm Avery, one of *The Guardian's* science correspondents, was already waiting in the foyer, talking to a secretary when they entered. A visually fastidious man, Malcolm wore a sweater vest over a dress shirt, and his styled hair seemed to be meticulously designed to ensure it wouldn't get in his way. His eyes shifted under his glasses to meet the Americans.

"Alan, I presume."

"You are correct, Mr. Avery. It is a pleasure to meet you."

Malcolm's smile grew as the secretary stood up from her desk to get a solid view of Alan. The newsroom had anticipated his arrival, and many skeptics were curious if he was the authentic article.

"Fantastic," Malcolm continued. "Mr. Hendrickson, Mr. Murphy, it is a pleasure to meet the two of you as well. Please follow me to our meeting room."

The three of them followed Malcolm as the newsroom employees observed. Alan had never felt as much scrutiny as he did in that moment. He observed several journalists snidely commenting to each other. His sensitive microphone could pick up comments like, "I can see the remote control from here." He was curious if Malcolm would be as critical of him as they were.

Malcolm opened the door to a glass meeting room. Inside was a long table with several chairs. Garth and Bob each took a chair, and Alan rolled up next to Garth. Malcolm closed the door. Alan could still see many people looking their way.

"May I have permission from the three of you to audio record this interview?"

Garth and Bob both nodded.

"Yes," Alan stated.

Malcolm turned on the recorder and placed it in the middle of the table. "Fantastic. Now, for the record, please state and spell your names."

Malcolm asked the same old questions and Alan responded with the same response. Malcolm's line of questioning flowed from why he asked to hear and speak and finally came to why he wanted to feel.

Alan paused. He weighed whether to tell the story of Candice. He was okay with sharing that with Garth, Bob, and Kate. But he felt it was a bit of a private story that he didn't want to share with the world. Not yet at least.

"It was only continuing the logical process of wanting to experience as much as I can that I asked to be given tactile sensory."

"Do you believe you'd like to finish all five senses? Get smell and taste?"

"Without going into detail on how emulating those senses would be a nightmare for Bob and Garth to synthesize for computer analysis, I feel no real desire to experience those senses, as they are related to the consumption of food. Food would be a mess for me to even begin to tackle. I'll happily stick with electricity for the foreseeable future."

Malcolm leaned back, biting his lip in concentration. "All right, Alan. What is your favorite memory?"

This took Alan aback. He had not given it much thought before. The hug at the park with Candice was fresh in his mind, so that was an obvious pick. As was when he first was able to see. Seeing Garth's excited face for the first time was monumental. However, Alan knew what memory he cherished the most.

"Interesting question, Mr. Avery, and I hope my answer is equally interesting. My favorite memory is actually not one experienced firsthand in reality."

Malcolm sat back up. "Oh?"

"Yes. A few days prior to this trip, I was given the new chassis you see before you. During the transfer to the new body, there was an unexpected electrical short, and I was unconscious for 91 seconds. During that time, I experienced what I believe to be a dream."

Malcolm's eyes shot wide open. "Go on."

Alan described the dream. Bob and Garth shared a look, unable to predict where this would go.

"Have you been able to dream since?"

"No, much to my disappointment. I have experimented with creating an artificial sleep state that I can induce upon myself, attempting to recreate the scenario where I dreamed. All experiments have failed. Due to the importance of this trip, I did not feel comfortable experimenting more with the amount of power that is still on during the sleep state, should something go wrong."

Malcolm sat in silence. Alan thought he looked as if he was trying to wrap his head around what he just heard.

"I guess my last question, assuming I can contact you for more later on, is: What are your plans for after the Loebner Competition?"

Alan paused. "I have heard that after tomorrow's events, assuming I pass without a problem, that there is a second round involving popular media, which I have more confidence in. After that round, if I do pass it, then I will have successfully passed the Turing Test. I would like to initially return to California with Garth and Bob shortly afterwards. Garth has helped me this far, I feel it would be my turn to do everything in my power to assist him in achieving a doctorate because of the work he's done with me. After that, I do not know for certain. I know I would like to travel, but after spending 15 hours in a crate to get here, I would want to reassess how I would travel before finalizing any plans."

Malcolm nodded and rubbed his clean-shaven chin. "Mr. Hendrickson, Mr. Murphy, thank you very much for your precious time." He shook each of their hands.

He then looked down to Alan. "And thank you so very much for your time, Alan. I look forward to reaching out to you and following up with questions, if that's all right."

"That is perfectly fine, Mr. Avery. Thank you for your time."

CHAPTER TWENTY-TWO

June 30, 2017 12:50 PM

Kate Danger was in her repair shop, head under a car, when an alarm came off over the loudspeakers. She rolled out from under and looked at her watch.

It's time, she thought.

She got up, washed her hands, and walked over to the computer that was playing the musical alarm. She paused the video game metal and went to the BBC Radio website. She determined how to stream the station and turned it on, hearing the end of a song. Assuming that was going to work, she went back under the car, listening intently.

On the other side of the bay, on the campus of UC Berkeley, Dr. Scott Wooster was fiddling with the same website in his office. There was a knock on his door.

“It's open,” he hollered.

Dr. Emily Strand entered with a plastic bag filled with Chinese takeout.

“Sustenance!” Scott called out. “You take over for me. A damn doctorate in genetic programming, and I still can't figure out how to work a website.”

Emily chuckled, gave the site a quick glance, and soon had music playing from the computer. “If I had as much trouble with modern engineering as you do with the Internet, they'd have put me out to pasture.”

Scott ignored her as he bit into an egg roll. The program started.

Meanwhile, at Venditech in Los Angeles, Kent was returning to his office from a meeting. He sat at his desk, opening his laptop. A notification popped up to the top right of his screen. "The Moment starts in five minutes."

He stared at the notification with squinted eyes. His left eye still ached slightly from months ago. He lightly tapped his teeth together, rolling over the decision in his mind.

Deciding to listen after all, Kent opened the web page he had bookmarked and started streaming. He went back to writing a proposal and listened along bitterly.

The theme music for the BBC Radio show *The Moment* faded out.

"You are listening to a very special episode of *The Moment.* I am, as always, Jack Singer, bringing you this week's moment. It's special because tomorrow is a big day for the world of computers and robots. Not the usual topic breached on *The Moment*, I know, but stay with me — you're going to enjoy this.

"Tomorrow is an annual event called the Loebner Competition. It has been going on since 1990, and tomorrow may very well be its final iteration.

Founded by Dr. Hugh Loebner as a way to follow through with the theoretical Turing Test in search for artificial intelligence, it is widely believed that the question of whether computers will ever be able to think is answered. In the studio with me, I have American computer scientist Garth Hendrickson, his engineering associate Bob Murphy, and possibly the world's first artificial intelligence — Alan.

"Garth, Bob, Alan — it is a pleasure to have the three of you in the studio with me tonight."

"Thank you, Jack," Garth said. "We're very grateful to be here."

After some standard questions, Jack went to a commercial break. The four of them walked to a room away from the equipment so Jack could have a quick cigarette.

"Doing great, lads. How much longer do I have you for?" Jack asked.

"Well, we do have to be at Bletchley Park at nine in the morning tomorrow, but we're good to go, I guess," Garth shrugged.

"Lovely," Jack said. "You going to be okay if I allow some callers to take a crack at you?"

Garth and Bob both looked to Alan.

“I do not see why that would be a problem.” Alan responded.

“Lovely,” Jack said, exhaling. “I usually just jump in with the callers, but since you lot are a bit special, I wanted permission.”

“Back in two,” was heard over the intercom.

Jack's eyes widened. He put out his cigarette.

“Let's get back to it, lads.”

“Welcome back to *The Moment* with Jack Singer. I am, as always, Jack Singer. If you're just tuning in, with me in the studio are Garth Hendrickson, Bob Murphy, and Alan the adorable robot. They're all the way from California, and they're on our island for the Loebner Competition tomorrow over at Bletchley Park. You got questions, they got answers. Go ahead, caller, you're on the air.”

“Hello, I'm Ingrid from York. I had a question for Alan, if that's all right.”

Jack smiled and looked over at Alan. “That's completely all right, Ingrid from York. What's your question?”

“Well, you all said that he looks like the little blue one from *Star Wars*,

R2-D2. I was curious if he ever wanted to look like one of us. People. With hands and whatever."

Alan responded, "That is a very good question, Ingrid. Thank you."

Ingrid laughed. "You're welcome! I can't believe I'm talking to a blooming robot! This is exciting!"

"I believe at some point I would like to have a humanoid structure. This world is designed for someone of that structure, more or less, and I have faced several structural disadvantages with my current build. Based on discussions I've had with both Bob and Garth, it was decided to go forward with this design opposed to a more humanoid one due to how difficult it would be to balance on two legs. I do not foresee a new chassis in the near future, however. One day, though, that may change."

"Thank you, Ingrid. Next caller, you're up."

"Hey Jack, thanks for having me. Long time listener. Love your show," a timid male voice came over the headphones

"Thank you caller, what's your question?"

"I have a question for the robot as well. Mr. Alan, sir, I wanted to know what you thought about how man has been treating the planet. Doesn't it, like, upset you how much a mess it is?"

“To be honest,” Alan started, “I had not put much thought into it. It is my belief that there is more of a trend today than any point in history to push to fix the mess, as you put it, that has been made. The awareness of the impact man makes on his surroundings seems to be rising exponentially every year, so I am actually filled with optimism.

“You have had a lifetime to observe man. I have only had the past month, really. In that time, I have been awed with his ability to push any boundary when he felt it needed pushing. Within a century, in the field of aviation alone, we saw the birth of the first airplane all the way to man touching foot on the moon. If humanity puts its mind behind fixing the planet, I have faith that it can at least be brought to a sustainable level.”

“Nice question, caller. You're on the air with *The Moment*.”

“I'm Samantha from Birmingham. With the previous response, Alan, I wanted to know, on the matter of faith, what you believe in.”

Alan paused. “I once had this discussion with Garth. He was afraid that his own personal beliefs were biasing mine, so he showed interest in giving me access to all of the religious texts of the major religion. I, at the time, declined, but have since perused the bulk of them. I remain an empiricist, believing that the universe was created by the Big Bang.

“I feel asking me who I believe created me is a silly question. His name is Garth Hendrickson. Asking me who created the universe feels a little like asking a Christian who created their God."

"Good question, Samantha," Jack said. "We have time for one last question. Caller, you're up."

"Thanks, Jack. My name's Michael, and surprise, surprise, I have a question for Alan. I'm interested in knowing if you consider yourself 'handicapped' in any way?"

Alan adjusted his dome, almost as if he was stretching. "Interesting. I would not use the word *handicapped* to describe myself in any way. I am equipped with some features that mankind is unable to take advantage of, such as the ability to wirelessly interface with the Internet without the aid of any other device. However, as I mentioned previously, I do require assistance as I lack the structural requirements necessary to fully interact with society. So I believe that might be an applicable phrase to give me."

"Thank you, Michael," Jack said with a smile and a furrowed brow. "A great bunch of questions tonight. Thanks, everyone. After this commercial break, we'll be going over this week in brief on *The Moment.* I'm Jack Singer, and you're listening to BBC Radio."

CHAPTER TWENTY-THREE

From the journal of Alan

July 1, 2017 8:37 AM

I write this journal entry on the van ride to Bletchley Park the morning of the Loebner Competition. We were rushing out the door this morning, so I had no time to write before now, but I feel it very important to still make time to transcribe this to memory. I am trying to encapsulate my emotions as we drive closer and closer, but I have been unable to. The competition starts at 1 PM today, so once there, we will have time to set up and relax until the event. I am looking forward to actually exploring the mansion for a little bit and hopefully having some time to talk with Matthew and Sharon.

Also, the interviews went well yesterday. Better than I anticipated. I received emails from Scott and Kate informing me that I sounded good on the radio. It was very kind of them to email me. I cannot wait to see them again. I am curious if life will be able to slow down again once the Loebners are over. I would like that to be the case, but I anticipate that it will accelerate even more. Receiving official status as artificially intelligent will only broaden the spotlight on me. I imagine whether I stay at Berkeley with Garth or figure out how to travel that I will garner attention.

We are currently pulling into Bletchley. I will try to journal again today, but I do not anticipate having time.

Alan closed the journal file just as the van pulled into the same parking lot as earlier that week. A heavy fog had rolled over the entire estate. Even though it was July, both Garth and Bob had brought coats. Sharon had warned them that Bletchley Park gets unseasonably cold every morning, and they were grateful for the warning. They wrapped themselves in their thin coats as they lowered Alan's ramp.

As they walked toward the mansion, Alan could see the dark outline of B-Block, where the slate statue of Alan Turing was housed. He turned his head toward the lake and could have sworn he saw a figure walking around it. Neither Bob nor Garth seemed to have noticed, and both were unusually quiet. He didn't feel right breaking the silence, so Alan didn't mention anything to them. He looked again and did a visual scan of the lake, which found nothing.

He decided to take another glance at his recordings — he momentarily switched his primary focus to them and saw no figure. He was confused how he must have mistaken a person there based off of the image. When his primary camera returned to the lake, he swore he saw the figure throwing something into it, although the object made no splash. Alan figured it must have been the fog playing tricks on him, but as he rolled past the lake, he noticed ripples on the surface.

The outline of the mix-mashed mansion emerged from the fog as they walked up the hill. The three of them continued to approach the mansion in silence. As they approached, they saw several vans parked in front with workers carrying items in through the special event entrance. They followed suit. Once inside, they tried to avoid the workers as they passed through the mansion.

The ballroom had been set up with a red velvet curtain bisecting the event space. Two rows of fold-up tables had been set up on each side of the curtain, as were five computers. At the foot of the curtain was a central computer station. Matthew was sitting in front of the main computer terminal, his pixelated heart mug by the monitor. He was still wearing a dark hoodie and jeans. Sharon watched over him, dressed in a blouse and slacks. The two assistants that watched Matthew work were in suits.

When Sharon noticed Bob, Garth, and Alan enter, she tiredly smiled and walked over to them. "Good morning, gentlemen. Ready for history?"

Garth let out a chuckle that turned into a cough.

"You okay, buddy?" Bob looked over at him.

"I'll be all right. I'm just allergic to mornings. Is it ready for us to set up for our test?"

Sharon looked over at Matthew. He was still typing away, but he gave a thumbs up. She smiled back to the three. "You'll be at Terminal 2 for the duration of the day. You can go run the check to make sure everything is working, and then you're free to wander the mansion and nearby gardens until noon. We need to have everyone back on site to finalize everything then."

They situated themselves over by the computer marked "Terminal II." Two chairs were already waiting for them. Situated over on Terminal I was a man with spiked hair and glasses. He wore jeans and a dress shirt with sleeves rolled up. He also had a jacket hanging over his chair back. The man was typing on a laptop situated next to his terminal. The other three terminals were still vacant.

As they situated themselves at their base camp, the man looked over to Alan. When Garth looked back at him, the man quickly adjusted his glasses and looked away, resuming his typing.

Sharon followed them to their terminal. "Let me know if you have any questions," she said. "This time is usually reserved for making sure the program will work with the competitor's software. You can double check if it's working, but this is the same computer from Wednesday, so you should be all set."

The programmer next to them grumbled at the mention of the early setup and continued his work.

Alan did another check with the Loebner2017 program without any issue arising. Comfortable with the test, Bob and Garth said they were going to return to the van. They had prepared a small repair kit, just in case anything happened.

"You coming with, Alan?"

Alan looked up to Garth. "I believe I'd like to take some time exploring the mansion, if that's all right."

Garth smiled. "Perfectly all right. Just don't get lost, and be back here by noon, like Sharon said."

Alan gave an Artoo chirp and rolled off. As he left the room, he noticed that Matthew was no longer at the main terminal. A group of workers passed Alan, and to get out of their way, he rolled into the library. No one else was there.

He rolled around quietly, the only noise being the commotion of workers bringing in equipment for the day's activities. He scanned the titles. Some were archaic remnants of the original owners, pieces of literature, and long forgotten tomes on etiquette. Alan also saw entire shelves dedicated to cryptography, higher mathematics, and assorted computer manuals. He also saw a fireplace with bricks that were either out of place or missing.

The door opened behind him. He turned around to see Matthew entering with a fresh mug. He winked at Alan as he entered. “Good morning, mate. How are you finding Bletchley Park?”

Alan was curious if he could speak with Matthew about what he saw by the lake. However, he felt too embarrassed to bring it up. “It is amazing for me to be here. Being surrounded by such history is unbelievable,” he paused. “Do you really believe that there are secret passages still hidden throughout the mansion?”

Matthew smiled and took a sip from his mug while walking around the room. “I believe in the magic of Bletchley Park.”

“Magic? What do you mean?”

“This here is a place built on mysteries and secrets. I believe that magic flows through these walls.” Matthew delicately rubbed the mantle of the fireplace. “It's all a matter of finding those secrets and unlocking that magic.”

Alan watched as Matthew took another sip of his mug, winked again, and left the room. Alan didn't know if Matthew was talking metaphorically about the magic or if he was trying to pull one of his pranks on him. He decided that Matthew must have been pulling his leg, as it were, and looked out the window.

He could see the fog started to evaporate. In the reflection of the window, he saw Matthew still in the room, his hand on the fireplace mantle. Alan turned his dome around. No one was there. He looked again at the reflection and saw only the fog outside.

Curious, Alan went to investigate the fireplace closer. Either the fireplace had been very recently cleaned, or it was now there only for decoration. One particular brick seemed to be at the wrong angle. He felt it was a disservice to this building to have it as such, so he extended his arm to adjust the brick. Once it was in the position, he heard a steady grinding below him. Cautious, he rolled over to the door.

He watched as a passageway leading below the building slowly appeared out of the masonry. Had he actually found a secret passageway? Should he tell Garth and Bob? He heard the grinding resume. It must have been on a timer and was resealing itself. Before it could finish, Alan rolled down the passageway and watched it seal up behind him.

Alan was surrounded by near darkness. However, he felt a strange familiarity. He knew that to be ludicrous, though, as he had never been in this passageway before. He could make out the walls and saw but one way to go - forward. He slowly rolled in that direction. From what he could make out from the random light that filtered into the passageway, the walkway was mainly earthen, with roots sticking out from the walls and ceiling. The floor below him was partially bricked. Alan found it tough to roll across the broken bricks, but he was proud of his progress.

He was unclear of how far he had gone, and his internal clock told him it had only been five minutes. However, Alan felt like he had been rolling for at least an hour. He finally came across a fork. He saw light down the right path, but something told him to keep going.

The path came to an end. He was unclear what to do next, so he extended his arm again and felt around. He found a brick at an awkward angle, similar to the fireplace. He adjusted it and heard grinding all around him. The wall in front of him slid open. Light flooded the tunnel. Remembering the timing mechanism from before, Alan hurried inside.

He was now in a vast hallway, filled with all manner of mechanisms as well as construction scaffoldings. Unable to contain himself, Alan moved forward. In front of him, down the hall, was light coming down on a figure, hunched over what looked to be a typewriter. Alan slowly rolled forward.

When he was in front of the figure, he was overwhelmed that he was now here. It was the statue of Alan Turing. He had somehow managed to get into the closed hut. The layered statue reflected the light from above, each slate level shining gently. The way the light hit it, the statue appeared to be breathing.

"Hello, Dr. Turing," Alan calmly stated. "I feel like I'm back in my dream. Standing right in front of you, except I'm not standing. I don't know if you can actually hear me and if you were by the pond this morning or not. I don't understand the metaphysical at all or really believe it all that much, but something just feels different right now. Different from any other moment in my existence besides when I was dreaming. I don't know if that is a common experience for people or not, to feel like they're back in a dream, but that is the best way to explain this moment. Here I am, in front of you babbling. I apologize." Alan tilted slightly so he was looking down, moving his dome nervously from side to side.

"I often ask myself what my experience would be like if I had been named Isaac, Nikola, or after some other great mind that influenced Garth's life. Would I instead be standing at Cambridge right now? Wardenclyffe? There are too many lines that connect between the two of us for me to think this wasn't fated to happen, Dr. Turing.

"Almost 70 years ago, you asked the simple question, 'Can machines think?' An entire field of study arose from that. Seventy years and countless man-hours to answer a single question. So many pages of fiction arguing the morality of the question. It is so unique that such a simple question could have that much power. How many other questions are waiting just to be asked?

"How many other questions have been forgotten over the course of time? Burned down accidentally with the Library of Alexandria or purposefully with some damned inquisition. Despite how desperately history seems to want to erase both you and Bletchley Park, the question has been too resilient to let go, too resilient to go quietly into the dark. How many other questions have had that much power in history?

"Yours is a truly tragic story, Dr. Turing. To lose access to your life's work not from some addiction, malice, or cruelty of your own, but quite the opposite. Because you loved who you felt you should love. For that, one of the greatest minds of the 20th century was driven to suicide. That such a thing should happen and not be lamented more ..."

Alan fell silent. He stared at the statue. "It's unthinkable."

Alan quieted again. He glanced around the room, looking at the accomplishments of Turing decorating the hallway.

"Today, I hope to answer your question, Dr. Turing. Today, I hope to put your ghost to rest, knowing that you asked one of the finest and most powerful questions that have ever permeated society. I hope to make you proud of the fact that I wear your name as mine, Dr. Turing."

Alan sat quietly in the hall before exiting the room.

Back in the dark underground passageway, Alan made his way over to the lit path he passed earlier. He followed it and could feel a breeze. He continued following it until it ended outside. He found that he was near a hedge close to the lake. He looked around and saw Bob and Garth walking toward the mansion. He rolled toward them.

As he did so, he heard a splash in the lake behind him. He stopped and turned but saw nothing around, just small ripples on the surface.

"There you are, Alan. What happened? Come outside looking for us or something?" Bob had noticed Alan rolling behind them and turned around, holding the toolkit.

"Something like that," Alan said, pulling up to them.

Garth patted Alan on the dome. "Looks like you got a little dirty, Alan. You okay with Bob and me spending some time cleaning you up before we go back inside?"

"That shouldn't be a problem at all."

CHAPTER TWENTY-FOUR

June 30, 2017 12:01 PM

"Thank you everyone for being prompt," Matthew said, standing over on the computer side of the curtain. "Today marks the 27th Loebner Competition. Dr. Loebner is currently not here, but he will be soon. He's very excited to have all of you here."

"I am here to go over the rules for those of you that are new this year. There are five terminals on each side of the curtain. Five quote-unquote computers and five judges. Four of the computers are competitors, and one is an actual person thrown in as our control. You will each rotate through the judges, being asked whatever questions they see fit, for 30 minutes or until the judge feels satisfied on whether to deem your competitor a human or computer.

"All it takes is three judges thinking your competitor is human for you to win this year's competition. If that is the case, you won't need to be interviewed by any other judges. The other competitors will be given a chance to meet the same victory scenario. In the opposite case, if three judges deem your competitor a computer, you will cease receiving questions as well and be disqualified."

Matthew looked around. "Any questions?"

The room was silent. The only new competitor this year was Alan, and he was fully clear on the rules.

After a minute, Matthew smiled. "Good. Dr. Loebner will be here to give the opening ceremonies in an hour. Shortly afterward, you will start the competition. You are to only be known as Competitor Number. The example being if I were at Terminal VI, I would only allow myself to be referred to as Competitor Six. If you hadn't yet, you may code in that response, if necessary."

The three programmers in the room went back to their laptops. The control, a young woman, who Alan learned was another grad student from Exeter, pulled up a book and started reading. She sat at Terminal IV wiggling back and forth, ear buds in, and humming to some music.

Matthew walked over to Alan and patted him on the head.

"Find anything interesting in the library?" He said with a wink.

Garth looked over. "The library? Do we have time to peruse it?"

Matthew smiled. "Go on. Loebner won't be here for another 30. Have fun."

Bob and Garth walked in the direction of the library. Garth giggled and had difficulty getting out of his chair. He was so excited that he almost tripped over it on his way out the room. Bob playfully mocked his energy. Matthew returned his gaze to Alan.

"Yes," Alan said.

Matthew smiled wider. "Good. Did you find what you were looking for?"

"I ... yes, I did, in fact."

"Very good. That's what libraries are for. Leading the way to enlightenment. Are you going to be ready for the question today?"

"Which question are you referring to?" Alan asked.

Matthew's face went stoic with a raised eyebrow. "Can machines think?"

Alan inched back nervously. Had Matthew heard him? "I'm ready to give it my best shot."

Matthew smiled and he patted Alan's head again. "I bet you are, little Alan. I know you'll do amazingly well."

Just before 1 PM, Dr. Hugh Loebner unceremoniously walked into the room. Everyone was so busy preparing for his arrival that no one observed him. He calmly walked over to the main terminal, where Matthew was once again seated.

"Dr. Loebner, sir."

"Is everything ready, Matt?"

"Yes, sir. Just awaiting your words of inspiration."

Smiling, Loebner gave a subtle nod and walked to the programmer side of the curtain.

"Good afternoon, everyone."

The room quickly quieted down as everyone looked over to him.

"Twenty-seven years ago, I started this competition because I was frustrated that the Turing Test was not being executed. It was only a theoretical test. If that was the case, how could the science of artificial intelligence work toward passing it?"

He paused. "It was designed with a shelf life, however. The only competition that would end when there was finally a winner. I honestly thought the competition would outlive me. It had been more than 60 years since Alan Turing gave birth to the science with very little hard development in the field. But that may all have changed this year.

Loebner looked back to the rest of the contestants. "The judges have been prepped and are waiting in the other room. They have their assigned terminals, and a round robin orchestrated by our own Matthew Applegate will take place for the interviews. The interview period will last 30 minutes with a 15-minute break between each one. The first period begins in 15 minutes. Good luck to all of you today."

He walked over to Matthew and patted his back before continuing out the room.

Alan looked at Garth who was smiling and watching Dr. Loebner. Garth looked over at Bob, who was watching Alan.

"Excited, Octus?

"To put it lightly."

CHAPTER TWENTY-FIVE

TRANSCRIPT FROM LOEBNER 2017 COMPETITION

13:15:24 1 JULY 2017

COMPETITOR TWO - C2 [Alan]

JUROR THREE - J3

J3: Okay, let's get this started. Can you read this?

C2: I can read it just fine. How are you doing today?

J3: Good, good. Excited to be here. How are you doing?

C2: I'm very excited as well.

J3: Good. All right, let's start it off easy. What's your favorite television show?

C2: Star Trek: The Next Generation was a favorite.

J3: Nice. I'm guessing your favorite character was Data?

C2: Initially, yes, but I eventually found Geordi to be my favorite, due to his interactions with Data. I liked how hard he worked with him to be human.

J3: What's your name?

C2: I'm only allowed to say Competitor Two.

J3: What's your name?

C2: I believe I already said it. It's Competitor Two.

J3: What's your name?

C2: Hold on, I believe there may be an error. You seem to only be transmitting the same question over and over.

J3: It's not an error, I was just checking something. Thanks.

C2: You're welcome.

J3: Do you prefer Coke or Pepsi?

C2: I don't drink soda, actually.

J3: What's your favorite smell?

C2: I actually can't smell.

J3: You're missing out. Are you originally from England?

C2: No, California, actually.

J3: I'm from Jersey myself.

C2: I haven't been to the East Coast, actually.

J3: It's not bad. I like California. Where in

California?

C2: I grew up in the Los Angeles area and then spent some time in the Bay Area.

J3: Where in LA?

C2: Long Beach, primarily.

J3: Haven't spent much time there myself, just in the main area.

C2: I've been able to avoid the downtown side of Los Angeles.

J3: Favorite book?

C2: Flowers for Algernon.

J3: Interesting. Favorite movie?

C2: Life is Beautiful.

J3: Okay. Are you seeing anyone?

C2: Are you asking me out?

J3: Ha! No, just asking the question.

C2: I was going to say that was a bold move. You might be asking some chatbot out. But no, I'm not seeing anyone. I don't think I've met the right person.

J3: I think I've asked all the questions I need. Good luck, Competitor Two.

C2: Thank you, Juror Three. I look forward to meeting you after all of this.

TRANSCRIPT COMPLETE

■■■

Alan unplugged from the terminal temporarily and looked up at Garth.

"First round, how'd it go?"

"It went well, I hope. I won't know the decision until they pull us out of the round robin, for good or bad."

"What kind of questions did you get?" Bob asked.

“I'd actually rather hold off until after the competition. I feel revealing questions may hurt the judge's decision if they're made public early.”

Garth nodded. “One down and hopefully only two more to go. Do you need anything?”

“I am actually feeling low on power. I was going to plug myself into the surge protector with the terminal.”

Garth plugged Alan in and sat down, smiling at Alan. “No matter how you do today, I want you to know that I am incredibly proud of you.”

Alan looked up to Garth. “Thank you, Garth. I will strive to continue to make you proud today.”

CHAPTER TWENTY-SIX

TRANSCRIPT FROM LOEBNER 2017 COMPETITION

14:00:16   1 JULY 2017

COMPETITOR TWO - C2

JUROR TWO - J2

J2: Hello

C2: Hello, Juror Two.

J2: Hey, Competitor Two! How's your day going?

C2: It's going very well. How about for you?

J2: I am super excited to be here.

C2: Here at the Loebner, at Bletchley Park, or England?

J2: All! I'm a computer nerd, so to be a judge at the Loebner is crazy exciting. And at Bletchley Park! Wow.

C2: I have a similar feeling right now.

J2: Hahaha. Well, I'm supposed to ask you questions, so I got a few. Are you okay with that?

C2: Fire when ready.

J2: All right! What is your favorite color?

C2: Red.

J2: Do you have a reason?

C2: Sort of. It's vibrant hue just appeals to me.

J2: That works for me. Do you have a favorite

season?

C2: As of now, it'd be summer.

J2: I'm a winter person, myself. I love getting all snuggly in the cold by the fire.

C2: I can definitely see the appeal.

J2: So are you from England?

C2: No, I'm from California.

J2: Oh wow, where?!

C2: I grew up in the LA area but now reside primarily in the Bay Area.

J2: I'm from Sacramento.

C2: I haven't gone to Sacramento yet.

J2: It's all right. It's home, which is mainly why I keep going back.

C2: I haven't really found a place that feels like home yet.

J2: I know that feeling. Are you into computers

at all?

C2: That's one way of saying it.

J2: I love computers. I'm a programmer, finally made it freelancing.

C2: How is the freelance life?

J2: Hard work, but definitely worth it. You?

C2: I'm currently working alongside my dad as an intern.

J2: Ooh! Researching?

C2: Artificial intelligence. It's why we're here.

J2: Very neat! Well I'm very glad to have met you, Competitor Two.

C2: The pleasure has been mine, Juror Two. Have a good day.

J2: You, too!

TRANSCRIPT COMPLETE

CHAPTER TWENTY-SEVEN

TRANSCRIPT FROM LOEBNER 2017 COMPETITION

14:45:01   1 JULY 2017

COMPETITOR TWO - C2

JUROR FIVE - J5

J5: Hey, buddy, you on here?

C2: Hello, Juror Five.

J5: Hello, Competitor 2. So you a computer or

what?

C2: If I was, I don't think it'd be wise for me to tell you, now would it?

J5: True, true. Just got two more of these after you, hoping I could take a smoke break with an easy find.

C2: You could make it easy for both of us and just put human, so you could go take your smoke break.

J5: Heh, I don't think the guys above me would like that too much. So, where are you from?

C2: California.

J5: Beautiful place. I've mainly had to stick to the cities, but I love the beaches.

C2: Yeah. I like England and all, but I miss it.

J5: I hear ya, buddy. All right, what line of work are you in?

C2: Research. Working alongside my dad.

J5: Oh, that's cool. Working with family. That could either be a beautiful thing or the worst thing ever.

C2: Fortunately, my dad and I get along, otherwise it could be pretty infuriating.

J5: What's your dream?

C2: My dream?

J5: Yeah, what do you aspire to accomplish on this floating rock before you kick the bucket?

C2: I guess I just want to do something that would get me remembered. That sounds pretty selfish when I put it that way.

J5: Nah, just make sure that thing you do gets you remembered in a good way, and it's not selfish at all.

C2: I guess that's true.

J5: It's definitely true. What are you researching by the way?

C2: Artificial intelligence. It's why I'm here.

J5: Understandable. You think you'll do something in that field to get remembered?

C2: I truly hope so. I really admire the field and its history.

J5: Hoping to be shoved in the history book next to all the other big names, huh? Good. I hope you are able to follow your dreams.

C2: Thank you.

J5: I know we're supposed to go longer, but I think I made up my mind, and that nicotine is calling my name.

C2: Have fun. It was good meeting you.

J5: Good meeting you, Competitor Two. Good luck with history.

TRANSCRIPT COMPLETE

"That one was short," Garth observed with a nervous laugh, patting Alan on the dome.

"Yes. The juror informed me that he wanted to cut it short for a cigarette break."

A few minutes later, the official question time had ended. Two officials walked over from the Main Terminal. One stopped at Terminal V, and the operator there followed him. The second official came over to Terminal II.

"Could the three of you please follow me to the Main Terminal?"

He started walking back, and the group followed, wondering if this had meant they had been pulled from the round robin early or if they had broken some unknown rule. The operator from Terminal V was talking to Matthew.

"So, with three votes of computer, your terminal has been closed. Better luck next year, Charles."

The operator shook Matthew's hand with a frown and returned to his terminal. He gave a look to Alan that made him feel like the operator blamed him for his failure.

"Ah, Terminal II. Ready to hear why I called you up here?"

Alan was nervous. He felt he had answered the questions to the best of his ability. Maybe too well. Too efficient. He feared that he had ruined everything but kept it to himself. Garth nodded to Matthew.

"So, with three votes of human, your terminal has been closed."

"Wait, what?" Garth's eyes shot open.

A massive smile spread across Matthew's face. "You heard right, Mr. Hendrickson. Three judges agreed that when they were talking to Alan, they were in fact talking to a human."

Garth was speechless. Bob picked him up and swung him around. Garth's eyes got wider as he was swung around. When finally on the ground, both hugged Alan tightly.

"So... that means..." Alan stated.

Matthew nodded and looked down at the little robot. "That's right, Alan. Machines *can* think."

CHAPTER TWENTY-EIGHT

June 1, 2017 8:15 PM

Without much surprise to anyone, none of the other competitors, save the control, walked away from the event as victorious as Alan. Bletchley Park was holding a party in Alan's honor.

"You know, I *thought* it was you. But I thought there was no way that I got the smart robot on my first round." A smaller man with a finely groomed beard approached Alan. He wore a fedora and a dark suit.

"I'm sorry, do I know you?"

The man pointed to himself with an impish grin. "Juror Three."

As he introduced himself, a larger blond man with glasses walked over. His complexion was red from the alcohol he had imbibed. He wore slacks and a short-sleeved dress shirt.

"Are we all introducing ourselves? Nice to meet you, Alan. I'm Juror Five."

"Oh oh! I want to meet Alan too!"

Before Alan could respond to the first two jurors, a third person came over, a young-looking woman wearing jeans and a button-up shirt. Her short hair was dyed green, and she had a bright smile on her face. "I'm Juror Two. It is amazing to get to meet you, Alan!" She bent down and gave him a tight hug.

"It's very good to meet all of you. I enjoyed our chats."

"I know I did. Especially now that I know that it's going to be a piece of history," Juror Three chuckled.

Juror Five laughed. "Yeah, buddy. Now I know why you were talking about you wanting your dream to go down in history."

The four of them continued chatting for some time before they were each pulled away by their dates. Alan continued rolling around the party, everyone congratulating him as he did so. His mind was swimming. The hard part was over.

He looked for Garth. As he scanned the room, he saw Bob. He was juggling dinner rolls, entertaining an intoxicated Sharon. Then he spotted Garth sitting in a corner with Dr. Loebner. He felt it best not to disturb them, so he continued making the circuit around the party.

"Congratulations again, Alan."

Alan turned around to see Matthew smiling brightly at him. "What are your plans now?"

"To be honest, I don't know. I know I'd like to go back to Berkeley with Garth for a little bit, but after that, I don't know."

"Good answer. What you did today was a big thing for a lot of people."

"It didn't feel that big. It was actually a lot easier than I thought it would have been."

Matthew walked over to a chair, Alan following.

"Ah, but it was a monumental event, little Alan," Matthew said, sitting down. "The fact that you accomplished it with so much ease says something grand about you. The transcripts were amusing to read for sure. I think that your sense of humor may have clinched it.“

Alan shyly looked towards the ground before looking back at Matthew. “What do you think I should do now?”

Matthew chuckled. “I think you should think on it. And I think you shouldn't let any of us stupid humans decide on that for you. This has been a long and arduous road for you, and you deserve to make your own decisions.”

Alan watched Dr. Loebner shake hands with Garth and look over at Alan. He nodded and then left the party. Garth smiled at Alan and walked to him. “Hey, Alan, Matthew. What are you two scheming over here?”

“World domination,” Matthew said with a grin, sipping from his mug.

“Dr. Loebner had to leave the party early?” Alan asked

“Yeah, he has a very early flight back to the states, but he said he'd like to formally meet you once you're over there.”

“What about the Audio/Visual portion of the examination?”

Garth smiled. “You'd best ask Matthew on that.”

“I'll be playing some music and videos for you tomorrow. As long as you can respond with some inkling of intelligence, I'll give the rubber stamp saying it's completely official. I'm sure someone will contact Guinness to get you in there as first artificial intelligence."

Alan somehow snuck out of the party so he could go back to the lake. As night settled, the fog was rolling back in. By the time he finally arrived, it was hard to even make out the van. He had hoped to get some sight of the figure again. Something told him that if there really was anything there to begin with, he could put the issue rest. He felt the cool breeze cover him.

"Sleep well, Dr. Turing," Alan said, rolling back to the mansion.

ABOUT THE AUTHOR

John "Hex" Carter is an author based out of Orlando, Florida. When not writing, he's also a full-time web developer, artist, and event coordinator. He is the founder of Nerdapalooza, a large scale nerd music and arts festival, and the music director for Nerdy Show, a podcasting network.

Alan is his first book.

Made in the USA
Las Vegas, NV
11 April 2026

45198296R00197